# WHO ARE YOU?

# ANNA KAVAN

# WHO ARE YOU?

**PETER OWEN**
LONDON AND CHESTER SPRINGS

PETER OWEN LTD
73 Kenway Road, London SW5 0RE

Peter Owen books are distributed in the USA by
Dufour Editions Inc., Chester Springs, PA 19425-0007

This paperback edition 2002
© Anna Kavan 1963
© Rhys Davies and R. B. Marriott 1975

A catalogue record for this book is available from
the British Library

ISBN 0 7206 1150 4

Printed and bound in Great Britain by
Bookmarque Ltd, Croydon, Surrey

All day long, in the tamarinds behind the house, a tropical bird keeps repeating its monotonous cry, which consists of the same three inquiring notes. Who-are-you? Who-are-you? Who-are-you? Loud, flat, harsh and piercing, the repetitive cry bores its way through the ear-drums with the exasperating persistence of a machine that can't be switched off.

An identical cry echoes it from further away, calling out the same unanswered question, which is transmitted to other birds of the same species, until hundreds or thousands of them are shouting it all together. The ceaseless cries come from all distances and directions, from everywhere at once. Some are louder than others, or more prolonged; but all have the same infuriating mechanical sound, and seem devoid of feeling — they don't express fear, love, aggression, or anything else — as if uttered simply to madden the hearer. The intolerable thing about them is the suggestion that they are produced by machines nobody can stop, which will eternally repeat the question no one ever answers.

As probably they do in another dimension, to which the listener may be conveyed in delirium . . . until the ultimate nightmare climax . . . when suddenly everything stops . . .

The tamarind trees, old and huge, neither quite in nor quite out of leaf, tower over the house, creating a tantalizing illusion of shade, in this burning climate. But their sparse foliage and thin twisting branches cast only a confused net of shadow that gives no relief from the sun. The giant trees seem to exist principally as perches for the many brain-fever birds which, ever since dawn, have been hammering out their perpetual unanswered question.

Now the sun is low in the sky. Its dazzle catches the tops of the trees, which merge indistinguishably into one another, the birds invisible in the glare, among the tangle of spidery branches. All one sees is the tremendous size of the tamarinds, the web-like intricacy of their interlaced boughs, speckled with small, dry-looking leaves of no special colour.

Though built only a few years ago, the house below has already been touched by the galloping decay of the tropics, and is infested by rats and termites. Brick below, the upper storey stained wood, it looks vaguely neglected, and seems to crouch, beaten down by the heat, having been constructed without regard for coolness, its insubstantial walls cracking, its woodwork warped and bleached by the sun. A few banana trees grow almost touching the walls, and tufts of their long, narrow leaves poke through the glassless windows, when these are not covered by metal fly-screens or wooden shutters, several of which are defective, so that they hang crooked.

In the middle of the house a square porch shades the front door and the car standing there, its flat roof railed round as if it were meant for a sitting-out place, though, facing straight into the sun, it is useless for this purpose during the day. It overlooks, and is in full view of, the road, a dirt track with two deep parallel ruts worn by the wheels of the bullock carts which compose most of its traffic.

The bare, brownish compound dividing the house from the road is intended to be a garden, though nothing grows there but a single tall dilapidated palm tree in the middle. Its topmost leaves wave vigorously, with a clattering, almost metallic sound in occasional gusts of hot wind; but the dead lower leaves, which should have been removed, hang down in an untidy, decaying mass round the trunk. Beyond the road stretches a disorderly terrain, confusing to the eye, which retains no clear impression of it. Here the plain meets stony, scrub-covered hills, invaded by spearheads of jungle, spreading down from higher hills in the background. A group of great forest trees, entangled in creepers as thick as an arm, creates a sudden black area of shade on the right of the house, but unfortunately this doesn't reach anywhere near it. To the left is a swamp, full of snakes and leeches, covered by the large, bright green platters of fleshy plants growing in the treacherous mud these leaves conceal.

As the sun sets, colour drains visibly from the sky, against which the treetops behind the house, freed from dazzle, suddenly stand out clearly in all their intricate complexity. It should now be possible to see the brain-fever birds, which at last are silent. However, they remain invisible, either because their immobility makes them indistinguishable from the involved pattern of the branches, or because they've already flown off to different roosting places.

Far more striking than their non-appearance, is the abrupt cessation of their nerve-racking cries. The eternal, monotonous question without an answer has woven itself into the whole fabric of the day, and even now still leaves behind it a soundless echo, like some obscure irritant of the mind.

Daylight vanishes in six minutes flat, leaving only a faint violet smear marking the western sky. Stars flash out one after the other. In the swamp, frogs have begun making a great noise, which steadily grows louder, an incessant chorus of croaking, gulping and barking sounds working up periodically to a climax, when it is called to order by the punctuation point of a startlingly deep, gruff, batrachian boom, louder than all the rest, after which the cycle builds up again.

The moon has not yet risen. Only a faint ghostly sheen of starlight hovers over the marsh. The house is to be heard rather than seen, its timbers emitting cracks like pistol shots as the air cools and the faulty structure contracts and subsides. A thin pencilling of horizontal light-lines marks the position of windows. Two, longer than the others, open on to the flat roof of the porch, and through these a young girl emerges, advancing towards the rails — they cut her off at the knee seen from below, as she leans upon them. The light from inside the house isn't bright enough to show the colour of her dress, which is probably white.

She raises both hands and lifts her hair for a moment to cool her neck, then lets it fall and again leans on the rail. She is quite motionless, leaning forward slightly as if trying to see something on the ground below; which is impossible, the darkness being impenetrable down there. Her hair, no darker than her dress, hangs almost shoulder length in a long, childish bob, unskilfully imitating the style known as ' page boy '.

The racket the frogs are making doesn't drown the exasperating cry of the brain-fever bird, which has crept right into her head. Divorced from its cause, this lingering irritation is able to attach itself to anything in the dark, where nothing is distinguishable from anything else. She associates it in turn with the heat, the frogs, and then with the jingle and flickering gleam which would be the sole evidence of a passing bullock cart, if the driver did not keep up a loud chanting to protect himself from the demons of the swamp.

The girl never moves an inch; does not look round when a dignified barefooted servant, with a white turban and a grey beard, comes to the window behind her. She hears him, but gives no sign. And he, having watched her inscrutably for a while, withdraws in silence, glancing back disapprovingly from her to the open windows, through which clouds of mosquitoes and other insects are streaming continuously, attracted by the light inside.

Around the bare electric bulb, which the white saucer-shaped shade does not hide, they circle in ever-increasing density, almost obscuring its light. Their numbers make them unrecognizable in flight, as they are in death, and their scorched, charred, singed, or still spasmodically twitching bodies pile up on the tabletop and finally overflow on to the bare unpolished floorboards beneath. Here they are hidden by the table's circular shadow, though a few feebly and lop-sidedly drag their maimed legs, fire-shrivelled wings, and broken antennae some inches further, before they finally twist into lifeless shreds of detritus.

Waited upon by the disapproving servant, the husband is eating his dinner in the dining-room. The girl has stayed on the roof where it's cooler. It's not unusual these days for the meal to be served and eaten without her. Since the hot weather started she has no appetite. She has not been long in the country, and her constitution is not yet adjusted to the torrid, unhealthy climate. Besides, the pair have nothing in common; although they have only been married a year, neither enjoys the company of the other.

The man has a curious inborn conviction of his own superiority which is quite unshakeable. All his life he has bullied and browbeaten those around him by his high-and-mightiness and his atrocious temper. As a boy he terrorized his entire family by his tantrums, when, if thwarted, he would throw himself on the floor and yell till he went blue in the face. It has been much the same ever since. Everyone's terrified of his rages. He has only to start grinding his teeth, and people fall flat before him.

His wife is the only one who doesn't seem to succumb, which of course annoys him. Besides, he has other things against her : such as her not being a social success, and her inability to run the house efficiently. Actually, she's as out of sympathy with domestic and social affairs as he is with intellectual pursuits, and scarcely attempts to control their numerous servants of different races.

Some of these have been in the master's service before his marriage and resent her presence, putting the others against her and deliberately making her inefficiency more obvious.

The man in the dining-room is aware of all this, as he is of the significance of the fact that his dinner is being served, not by the butler who must have been forced to give up his place, but by his own personal boy. The severely ascetic grey-bearded Mohammedan has been with him ever since he first came out here as a junior. Of course his position now is much higher, but he has a perpetual grievance because it's not higher still, and considers that he's unfairly treated, passed over instead of promoted, unaware of the extent to which arrogance and bad temper prejudice his advancement.

His boy occupies a privileged place in the household, not only because he's been with him longer than anyone, but also because waiting upon his person implies a certain intimacy, as his presence now indicates. He knows all is not well between his master and the young wife, whose neglect of her domestic duties on which his comfort depends is typified by her leaving the windows open, so that the house is full of mosquitoes. It is to show his sympathy, and his wish to atone for her deficiencies, that he is in attendance — so anyway he wants the other man to believe — wearing his huge, heavy, elaborately wound turban, instead of taking his ease and enjoying the ministrations of his own properly subservient wife.

It is true that the master relies upon him, perhaps more than he knows. He would prefer to employ only Mohammedans, regarding them as more trustworthy than the local people, and only does not do so because government policy is against such discrimination. He dislikes the volatile inhabitants of the country, seeing them as irresponsible and amoral, their natural gaiety offensive to his puritanism. He is always at pains to be scrupulously fair in his dealings with them, but his attitude makes itself felt, and arouses hostility. However, as the natives are lighthearted and not much interested in the white people, their antagonism is expressed mainly in the form of mockery and they have named him Mr Dog Head — one doesn't at once see why.

Aggressive and overbearing physically as well as by nature, his arrogance makes him look taller than he really is, lean, muscular, tough and bony, with bright blue eyes that can flare up like rockets. The reddish tinge of his close-cut hair has been lightened by exposure to the tropical sun, and it clings to his skull like short fur. Without being exceptionally hairy, his arms share this close pelt, which appears to cover his whole body. Although he wears neither tie nor jacket, his shirt is immaculate, and he has changed for dinner into white trousers, instead of the shorts he wears during the day.

He eats fast, like someone who has to catch a train. Of course he conveys the food to his mouth silently and in the orthodox way; yet his jaws seem to close with a snap, he is already busily collecting the next mouthful with his knife and fork while still masticating the last. Nevertheless, it would be distinctly far-fetched to say there was any resemblance to a hungry dog in the eagerness with which he consumes whatever is on his plate, leaving it perfectly clean.

Mosquitoes are starting to penetrate into the room. It's impossible to keep them out as there are no doors, only wooden panels fixed to the door frame, so that air can circulate freely. Mohammed Dirwaza Khan has stationed a couple of boys outside with orders to hold up a net from wall to wall. But their arms are aching, they feel they've been most unfairly conscripted for this extra job, and they begin muttering rebelliously in voices that reach the diner's sharp ears.

He catches the eye of his servant, who is already moving to clout them into obedience, and just perceptibly shakes his head. He has finished. Pushing away his plate he stands up, ignoring the pink confection served for dessert as a traditional concession to the supposed sweet-tooth of his wife — he never touches it. On the way out he smiles at the Mohammedan, briefly showing his teeth; large, white and strong, they suggest a wolf more than a dog.

Throughout the meal he's said not a word to the man. Since he still doesn't speak and only smiles at him in passing, it's hard to say why he now seems to show more than the normal goodwill towards him — almost familiarity — or how his smile exceeds the permissible, or fails to comply with conventional standards of conduct, or appears indiscreet.

The recipient of the smile notes the slight excess — if that's what it is — with gratification. It accentuates the perfection of *his* behaviour in acknowledging it only by bowing his head, without overstepping formal correctness or discretion in the slightest degree. In fact, an on-looker would see no difference between this salutation and the bow he invariably makes when his master passes on his way out of a room.

All the same, he is satisfied that his leisure has not been sacrificed in vain. And in future he will be more of a tyrant to the rest of the staff, because of the strengthened solidarity he feels with the man who has just left him.

## 5

The upper floor of the house is divided into three: a middle room into which the stairs lead, and a bedroom on each side. The bedrooms too are without doors, each door frame provided with two wooden panels which spring back into place after being pushed apart, a foot or two of vacancy above and below.

The central porch with its flat roof is reached by long windows from the middle room, which contains some cheap cane furniture and a larger piece that seems to have overflowed from one of the bedrooms. This is a wardrobe, made in the local jail, out of some dark reddish wood which always feels slightly sticky to the touch. Bottles, glasses and siphon stand on a table. In the middle of the ceiling a big fan circulates sluggishly, stirring up the hot air.

The wire screens are now closed over the windows and seem to exclude any coolness there might be outside. Yet the girl sits as close as possible to one of the windows, straining her eyes to read by the inadequate light from a bulb dangling far above; she can't bear to switch on the table lamp, which gives out more heat than light.

Mr Dog Head, a rolled-up newspaper in one hand and a wire fly-swatter in the other, prowls round the walls, methodically exterminating mosquitoes. There are so many of them that their high whine is audible above the whirring of the fan and the sound of his movements.

He realizes that he'll never be able to kill them all

and suddenly becomes exasperated, though not so much by the mosquitoes as by the girl's silence and immobility, and by the way she's taking no notice of him. It always irritates him to see her sitting about reading; that she should go on even when he's in the room seems a deliberate insult. His lordliness affronted by her lack of attention, he makes a wild swipe, simultaneously muttering something like, ' It's really too much . . . ', which he alters to an accusing : ' Is it too much to ask you to keep the screens shut ? ' gazing accusingly at her.

To his wife, there seems no point in answering. She feels that it's utterly futile to try to talk to him. She might as well talk to the wall, for all the possibility of communication between them. She keeps her eyes fixed on her book as though too absorbed in her reading to hear him.

Into her continued silence, he ejects : ' *Anopheles!* How many times have I told you they're deadly to me ? ' Identifying a mosquito by its trick of standing on its head, legs crossed over its back, as it hovers with wings extended, he crushes it with the paper, adding one more to the innumerable brownish blood smears on the wall. ' That devil's had somebody's blood already ! ' He again looks at her accusingly, as if she were to blame. As she's still silent, apparently absorbed in the book, he becomes determined to make her attend to him, demanding indignantly : ' Do you *want* me to go down with malaria ? '

' No, of course not.' She sees that she can't put off talking to him any longer, and reluctantly raises her head, confronting his angry face; it looks to her hard, blank and impenetrable as a wall, with two blue glass circles for eyes above the hard, almost brutal mouth.

What possible contact can she have with the owner of such a face? It half frightens her. (After all, she's only just eighteen, and he's double her age.) Feeling bewildered and helpless, she wonders why she's been pushed into marrying him.

'Have you taken your quinine?' is all she can find to say. She deliberately makes her face blank to hide her apprehension, with the result that she looks almost childish, her badly-cut hair hanging down by her cheeks. Her eyes are slightly inflamed by the glaring sun, and from trying to read in a bad light, and she keeps rubbing them like a little girl who's been crying.

Her words irritate him almost as much as her pale face, with its faintly bloodshot eyes, the vague, blank expression of which makes him angry because it seems so insulting, as though she were miles away. He too wonders why they are married; why did he ever allow her mother to persuade him into it? He feels he's been tricked — which isn't far from the truth. But none of this is clear in his head; he is only aware of the inflaming of his permanent grievance against life in general, and her in particular. He blames her for everything. She gets on his nerves so much that he moves his hand as if he meant to hit her, deflecting his aim at the last moment and squashing another mosquito instead.

A clock downstairs strikes ten. He counts the strokes, and is suddenly overcome by the emptiness of the evening. It's still quite early, and there's nothing on earth to do. More aggrieved than ever he stares round the room, and seems to be listening. Not a sound comes from below. The servants have finished their work and retired for the night to their separate quarters. If he wants one of them now he will have to shout and go on shouting for some considerable time. He is left with the noise the frogs are making outside, the mosquitoes, and the exasperating girl. What's the good of a wife who's no sort of companion? It doesn't occur to him that he's in any way responsible for their marriage. He blames her totally for not appreciating the privilege of being married to him.

Meanwhile how is he going to pass the time? Of course, he can get into his car and drive round to the club. But that's only another form of empty boredom. As he doesn't play bridge and dislikes the other men, knowing he's unpopular with them, all he can do there is drink. He might as well do that at home.

Swinging round to the bottles he pours himself a stiff whisky, swallows it, and immediately pours out another, not bothering about his wife, who never drinks. He remains standing, keeping his back to her, saying nothing. He goes on drinking steadily, trying to drink away his boredom, only occasionally interrupting the process to swat another mosquito.

The girl watches with more open apprehension. But she seems more alive; she has thought of something, and is only waiting for the right moment to put her plan into operation. When he notices something of interest on the bloodstained page in his hand and smooths it out, bending over to read, she stealthily gets up and tiptoes towards her room behind him, keeping her eyes on his back.

The husband knows all the time what she's doing, and just as she gets to the door suddenly jumps on her, shouting, ' Oh, no, you don't! ' seizing her wrist so violently that she utters an exclamation of pain, or fright, or disappointment, or all three, but doesn't speak a word.

His blue eyes blaze furiously at her. For some reason he takes her silence now as a sign of conceit, just as he does her continual reading — it's because he hardly ever reads anything but a paper himself that this seems like flaunting conceit and superiority. How dare she pretend she's superior to him, just because she's passed some damn fool exam women shouldn't be allowed to go in for? But what can he do about it? Inwardly raging in his frustration he stands gripping her wrist, until a gratifying idea comes into his head — he'll show her . . . ! He'll take the conceit off her face . . . !

His expression suddenly gloating, he orders, ' Don't move ! ' and hurries off, coming back the next moment with a couple of tennis racquets and thrusting one into her hand.

She accepts it unwillingly, opening her mouth as if to protest, but in the end says nothing. Several seconds later she is still standing in the same position, as if paralysed, the racquet dangling from her hand. He gets on with his drinking, but is careful to make no noise now, all the while listening and watching as well. It's obvious that both of them are waiting for something to happen, which she dreads, and he's looking forward to eagerly. Presently the whisky he's drunk seems to improve his mood, for he speaks to her more amiably, as if in encouragement, his voice only slightly above a whisper. ' Come on, now ! Be a sport — it's all good clean fun . . .' However, the low tone sounds furtive, with an underlying viciousness far from friendly. The girl is not taken in, but seems unable either to speak or move, just standing there, her eyes dilated and horrified.

All at once she gasps loudly. He silences her by a violent gesture. With disagreeable suddenness, as if from nowhere, a small animal has appeared in the room, its head and sensitive twitching nose turned towards them, its body foreshortened. Moving with the same disconcerting and rather unpleasant suddenness, it darts out of sight, reappearing halfway up the wall, where it is seen to have a long tapering leathery tail, like a whiplash, before it vanishes somewhere on the periphery of the ceiling; in the centre of which the fan continues to rotate as if nothing had happened, churning up the oppressive air.

The girl's eyes, which have been following the beast's movements, now return to her husband. She doesn't speak, has not moved, but, since she gasped, her lips have not closed completely and are now trembling, her breathing is faster than usual. She controls herself up to a point, but can't hide her aversion to this whole procedure, standing petrified, staring at him with wide eyes. He doesn't speak or move either, but watches the ceiling intently; both are virtually frozen. The room fills with suspense, with the noise of insects, and the drone of the fan.

Suddenly a confused scuffling above is followed by a squeal, cut off in the middle; a small animal — not the same animal as before — falls to the floor with a plop. Stunned, the rat lies still for a second, then picks itself up and rushes away. The man watches, estimating the distance with narrowed eyes, before swinging the racquet down and hitting the beast fair and square, sending it flying in her direction. ' Go on — lob it back to me ! You can't miss such an easy one ! '

Her fingers clench spasmodically on the handle of the racquet she's holding, but instead of obeying she lets it fall on the floor with a clatter, and drops her face in her hands.

'Oh, so you won't play . . .' His voice now has an ugly sound. But he's more interested in the rat, skidding sideways across the boards as fast as its injured legs can move — he brings the racquet swooping down on it very much faster.

Standing there triumphant, he pulls out his handkerchief and rubs the strings, while at the same time his foot heavily and repeatedly stamps on the thing on the floor, finally kicking it out of sight under the wardrobe. To horrify the girl even more he says spitefully, without looking round, 'Perhaps the rat king will come next,' referring to a legendary monstrosity consisting of six or eight rats (a whole litter presumably), joined together by a single tail. There is no reply. He goes on cleaning his racquet. And when he presently turns his head she is no longer there.

## 6

Mr Dog Head, quite nude, is inspecting himself in the mirror in his room, but as it is only big enough to show him down to the waist he is dissatisfied and keeps turning and twisting in an attempt to see more. The tough male muscularity of his body is now very apparent. And it is quite true that most of it is covered by the close brown-red pelt, resembling the neat covering of his skull, and that this greatly increases his doglike aspect, which the local people must have divined by instinct, since he's certainly never allowed them to see him naked.

This room is even barer than the one next to it. There is a single bare bulb dangling from the ceiling, the fan, the bed shrouded in dingy netting, a table beside it with a shelf underneath. On the top of the table is a whisky bottle, a siphon and a glass; on the shelf below lies the only book he ever reads, which can't be seen very well because it is in the shadow cast by the tabletop — black, it might be a bible, and is certainly a religious book of some kind with a gilt cross on the cover.

As he gazes at his reflection his big aristocratic nose seems to arch itself in arrogant complacency, as though he were lord of the earth. He does belong to a titled family, and if several people die first he will eventually become an earl. But this doesn't seem to justify his assumption that he's superior to everyone else alive and that everyone must give way to him.

Physically, he is quite impressive, in an overbearing fashion, flexing his powerful muscles that bulge and slide under the skin like bunches of snakes as he stretches his arms and bends several times to touch his toes. Even now, in the middle of the night, with the temperature at its lowest, this effort leaves his neck, arms and face thickly beaded with sweat; which, however, is quickly absorbed by the furry covering, quickly disappearing.

His big-nosed face glides over the mirror in profile as he stoops down, scrutinizing his legs, assuring himself that their muscular development is as satisfactory as that of his arms. He swings his weight from one foot to the other and pinches his calves, which are hard as iron. But, still not quite satisfied, he wants to see the whole of himself, and because he can't is suddenly overcome by his usual grievance against the world, his haughty countenance taking on a petulant look it must often have worn when he was a spoilt little boy. Impulsively he slops whisky into the glass, not bothering to watch how much he pours out, and gulps it down without adding any water. As if the spirit took effect instantly, he at once goes into the deserted middle room, which is faintly lit by the light in the room he has just left.

Tough as he is, and stark naked, he feels uncomfortably hot and pauses by the window, scratching his sticky scrotum, wondering whether to make the effort of opening the screens. At the sound of a mosquito sailing past his ear he decides against this, clutching furiously at the insect; but when he opens his clenched fist nothing is there. His sense of grievance increased by the mosquito's escape, he goes on and pushes through the panels into his wife's room, which contains the only full-length mirror in the house.

There is total darkness and silence in here. Although this is only what he expects, he's held up for a moment, stopping just inside the spring flaps of the door. His eyes quickly accommodate themselves to the blackness. He makes out the paler shadowy blur of the mosquito net over the bed, and, near it, something like a huge shining eye, which is the glint of the looking-glass on the wall. He calls the girl's name, and, getting no answer, calls again, more loudly and aggressively, adding : ' Come on — you can't fool me ! I know you're only pretending to be asleep ! ' Still there's only silence, which seems more profound after his interruption.

He now feels both violent and slightly muzzy, which is the maximum effect alcohol has upon him. He is far from clear in his own mind whether it is his wife or the mirror he wants, and means to have, but, as both are in the same direction, he takes a step forward, at once colliding painfully with a chair. Bursting into floods of obscenity, he stands rubbing his shins. From the bed there is still no sound — there might be nobody in it. This thought emerging from his muddled brain, he starts forward to investigate, having already forgotten the chair, into which he stumbles again.

' You put that there on purpose to trip me up ! ' he shouts accusingly and, as it happens, correctly. Then, gripping the chair in one hand, he swings it high in the air, and, without aiming precisely at anything, hurls it across the room. A tremendous crash follows, and then the prolonged tinkle of falling glass. The chair has crashed into the mirror and smashed it to smithereens, which sobers him up slightly. He feels a fugitive, remote guilt connected with the destruction of the glittering eye on the wall. Now that it's gone, as no sign of life comes from the bed, there seems no reason to stay in the room any longer. He turns, feels his way out between the panels, crosses the central room, and retires into his own.

Except for an occasional deep barking boom, the frogs are now quiet outside. The night is more than half over, but it's still as hot as a furnace, black and oppressive, as all the nights are. Its silence, which is no silence, but a pulsating of countless insects, is now and then disturbed by the cry of some unspecified animal, and punctuated more regularly by that batrachian booming.

Under the mosquito net the naked figure, with its fur-like covering, lies sprawled, flat on its back, legs splayed wide for coolness and the soles of the feet on view, black with dirt from the floor. Sleep has suddenly overtaken the man, whose head, just off the pillow, is tilted back, with the mouth half open. His hands lie loose and relaxed at his sides, having relinquished the objects they held when sleep overwhelmed him. The glass has lodged in the grimy folds of the net, stained by the blood of endless intruders and now also by the dregs of whisky the glass contained. The book has fallen face down from his other hand, where he opened it at random and was overcome by sleep before he could read the words he wouldn't have taken in anyhow. Cover upwards, the tarnished cross upside down, its thin pages are crumpled and folded in deep creases which will never come out.

The light, forgotten, burns on in the silent room, in the midst of the circling suicidal throng of creatures attracted to it.

## 7

Ever since sunrise the brain-fever birds have been calling out their perpetual question, and now the full power of the sun is relentlessly pouring down heat on the burnt-up land, which has hardly had time to cool off during the dark hours.

The girl stands at her window, looking over the marsh. This flat sea of swampy ground, covered with large fleshy leaves, extends to the very edge of the compound, separated from it only by a ramshackle fence, beyond which is a footpath, built up above the mud. She has watched, either on this path or the road, first, a silent, ghostly sunrise procession of yellow-robed priests with their black begging-bowls; then various groups of brown people with flowers behind their ears, bringing offerings to the giant sacred snake that lives in the tall forest trees, left standing when the land was cleared for building the house. (Though gigantic, this reptile is harmless, gorged on the birds and small animals presented to it, which it consumes alive, and is usually to be seen among the lower branches, its pallid length looped and dangling.) A party of little men from the hills has also trotted by, carrying loads of bananas to some distant market.

The last person to use the marsh path was a white man, quite young, wearing the regular tropical uniform of bush jacket and shorts, with the addition of soft leather mosquito boots. Every day he passes four times, coming from and going to his place of work. The girl has a fellow feeling for him because of his youth : he hasn't been out here long enough to lose his fresh complexion; his face has not yet hardened out of its youthful sensitivity. Because of the distinctive item of his attire, she always thinks of him as ' the man in suède boots,' and knows he won't appear again now before midday. But, paralysed by the heat, she still stands gazing out at a patch of black ooze between the bog plants, where iridescent shimmers reflect the sky. Probably it's because she can't get used to the climate that she feels so strange all the time, and can't get used to her life in this country either.

*Is* it her life? It hardly seems so. A picture comes to her of her schoolfriends, enjoying themselves in pretty dresses and gay surroundings, or else at the university, as she ought to be. Who *am* I? she wonders vaguely. Why am I here? Is she the girl who won the scholarship last year? Or the girl living in this awful heat, with the stranger who's married her for some unknown reason, with whom it's impossible to communicate? Her questions remain unanswered; both alternatives seem equally dreamlike, unreal. Somehow she seems to have lost contact with her existence . . .

She gives up the problem, and, in a gesture become automatic, raises both hands to lift the hair off her neck — the dampness of the flesh makes her aware of the sweltering heat (these upper rooms with their wooden walls are uninhabitable during the day, no better than ovens), and that it's long past the time when she generally hears her husband drive off to his office, a fact she's half consciously been ignoring. Deciding reluctantly to find out what's happening, from force of habit she first picks up a comb, but immediately drops it as it is to hot to hold. Then she goes out between the wooden flaps, which spring back into place behind her.

In the second room, her eyes avoid the wardrobe made in the jail, and keep to the floor, which is covered in stains, almost as if she were looking for a special mark. This is how she suddenly finds herself about to collide with a barefooted youth in a white turban, who is being trained as Mohammed's successor, and has just silently climbed the stairs with a jug of water. The normal course of his duties does not bring him up here at this hour, so she makes a perfunctory effort to assert herself by asking what he is doing.

The jug prevents him from putting his palms together in a formal salute, so he bends his head, making the obeisance as mechanically as he performs any trick he is taught — it seems no more a sign of respect than of any other feeling, or of none. ' Master, he has fever.' Devoid of expression, his big black eyes appear depthless, almost like those of an animal, as he gives the information with no trace of feeling.

All the servants look at her in this blank way that hides their feelings and thoughts—if they have any. This particular boy speaks good English, but arranges his sentences oddly, and announces all news, regardless of whether it's good or bad, in the same flat voice, as though the words have no meaning for him.

The girl precedes him now into the third room, which the sun hasn't reached yet, so that a very faint trace of the night's comparative coolness still lingers, combined with the stale smell of whisky. She stops just inside the door, astonished by her husband's sick face, which nevertheless contrives to look overbearing and extremely bad tempered, as he submits to the ministrations of Mohammed Dirwaza Khan, who is too preoccupied even to notice her arrival. In response to an order in his own language the youth puts down the jug, and departs precipitately. The bearded Moslem continues to pile blankets upon the bed; which so amazes the on-looker, who's never before witnessed an attack of malaria, that she allows some expression of incredulity, such as, ' In this heat . . . ? ' to escape from her unawares.

The patient hears, and, struggling up to confront her, bares his teeth in a sort of snarling grimace. ' Idiot! Can't you see I'm freezing to death? ' His teeth are, in fact, chattering loudly, convulsive shudders shake through him, his grimacing mouth can hardly bring out the words : ' Are you satisfied with what you've done? This is all your fault . . .'

' Mine? ' She stares at him, horrified, almost believing he's really about to give up the ghost.

' Yes, *yours!* Why did you have to let in all those mosquitoes? I've told you a million times they carry infection.' Falling back exhausted, he mumbles : ' You'd like to see the end of me, wouldn't you? '

' Oh, no! ' She's suddenly shocked into feeling sorry for him. ' I didn't mean . . . didn't understand . . .' But then she falters into silence, not knowing what to say.

The man is not in the least placated. He heaves himself up again, exposing his whole torso, to which the furlike hair is now damply clinging. Cursing incomprehensibly, he tries to throw off the covers, but the effort proves too great, and he collapses again, exclaiming weakly : ' Leave me alone! You make me sick! '

The girl hesitates for a moment, torn between a desire to escape, a feeling of guilt, and a mixture of repugnance and pity for the speaker, on whose face great drops of sweat are now starting out.

' Better missis go now.' The servant's voice has no trace of emotion, he doesn't even look round, still stooping over the bed. His large blackish hand, with its paler pink palm and fingertips, grasps a clean folded handkerchief, with which he gently and efficiently wipes away the sweat on his master's face, while the latter gasps : ' Yes — get out . . . and stay out ! '

A second longer she stands there unhappily, her feelings divided, listening to the monotonous voice murmuring soothingly as to a child as the big dark hands deftly smooth the blankets over the prostrate form, whose spasmodic shudders are still visible through the mass of bedclothes, accompanied by semi-delirious mutterings.

Who-are-you? Who-are-you? Who-are-you? Sudden and piercingly loud a brain-fever bird's cry sounds startlingly close, as if it were in the room, drowning all other sounds. Numerous birds all round the house call back the same question, and a whole explosion of identical cries breaks out on all sides at once.

The eternal Who-are-you? Who-are-you? Who-are-you? repeated from the tamarinds at the back, from the palm in front, from the trees where the snake lives, from the banana trees just outside, from the marsh, from the bushes screening the servants' quarters, and from further away, creates an exasperating din that seems as though it will really go on for ever. The ear-splitting, monotonous repetition continues like an infuriating machine-noise nobody knows how to stop.

All of a sudden the girl can't stand it; her clumsily cut hair swings forward abruptly as she covers her ears with her hands. The dreamlike reality in which she lives these days seems to be trembling on the brink of nightmare as she hurries out of the room, pushing open the wooden door-flaps with such force that they go on vibrating long after she's disappeared.

Mohammed Dirwaza Khan watches by day and by night. His main function is to watch over his master. His always watchful eyes and retentive memory observe and record all that takes place in the house and the compound. Fanatically jealous of the man's reputation, he defends him to the point of bloodshed against the slightest attack. A breath of criticism or even a joking remark can start a lifelong vendetta. His loyalty is blind, absolute; to the death he would serve his master, if necessary without payment. He lies, steals, intrigues, spies, bullies, fights, and possibly even murders for him; cares for him with endless unspoken devotion in health and sickness.

What happens to him when the other man goes on leave is a mystery. But, by some secret personal magic, he discovers the date and place of his return, and is there, waiting for him, at the airport or on the quay-side, ready to welcome him back with a profound salaam. After which he resumes his duties as if there had been no year-long interruption. How he has lived through the interval nobody knows or cares. The one certainty is that he has served no other master, and never will.

The marriage of the man to whom he is dedicated could not have taken place within his sphere of vigilance — he would have prevented it. The accomplished fact he can only oppose by stealth, determined it shall not last. He regards the girl as an enemy and a rival, to be disposed of as soon as possible. Yet it has been clear from the start that she is no match for him, hardly worthy to be called an adversary, so totally does she lack all qualifications for holding her own against him, not even the weapon of love at her disposal.

He despises her deeply for her inability to adjust herself to the climate or to control the servants; for letting him keep his authority unchallenged; for being timid and, to his mind, unattractive and skinny; because she is not popular with the other white people, doesn't give elaborate parties or do anything to enhance his master's prestige. Etc. Etc. The list is endless.

He has worked against her secretly all along, cunningly undermining her in his master's mind; disparaging her as a housekeeper, as a hostess — even as a wife, though he only employs hints on this delicate, dangerous ground, and slyly disguises his abysmal contempt, which would seem to insult the other's powers of selection.

The sun is now directly overhead, directly above the house. It is the hottest time of the day, when life seems suspended and the whole world lies gasping, waiting for relief from the scourge of heat. Heat has silenced even the brain-fever birds; even the noise of swarming insects is muted. Not a breath of air moves the tamarinds; the shadow of their thin branches and speckled leaves looks like a black net cast over walls and roof and gives no more shade. The sacred snake is coiled motionless in the recesses of the great trees. Their foliage, dense, dark, solid looking as if carved in stone, does not stir when one of the small green parrots sheltering there is struck down by the heat, falling like a tiny bright meteor to the ground, where ants will dispose of it within the hour.

There is no movement about the house. The only living being in sight is the chuprassi, stretched out on the back porch, his sash and badge of office beside him, his raised arms folded over his face, the black bush of beard jutting beneath the apex of a triangle of which the other two points are the tufts of black wire sprouting in his armpits.

In the blinding glare nothing moves, either in the house itself or in the compound, or in the untidy, village-like cluster of huts composing the servants' quarters, hidden by straggling bushes, where even the constant crying of children is hushed. A half-starved pi-dog is panting with its head in a patch of shade;

the only motion to be seen there is the bellows-like pumping of its skeletal ribcage.

The master of the house sleeps fitfully beneath his mosquito net, nervously watched by a turbaned youth squatting on his hams. The bearded Moslem, whose successor he is to be, is descending the stairs: his lean bare legs shut and open like blackish scissors, outlined against the white material hitched round his middle, the upper part of his body only a shade or two darker than his grey beard. Now, without making the slightest sound, he comes out on to the verandah, and turns his hook-nosed face to the left.

Here, on the shady side of the house, the girl is lounging on an old steamer chair, her bare legs hanging over the side, her bare arms reaching up to the chair-back; a position which lets the maximum amount of air touch her body. On her lap lies a letter, but she is not reading. It came some days earlier, and has already been read so often that its folds are starting to wear thin. She knows by heart what is written on the paper under the college heading, about it being a thousand pities she can't take up the scholarship she won last year — is it entirely too late to reconsider . . .? Isn't she rather wasting her talents in that primitive country known as the white man's grave?

She keeps the letter carefully hidden from her husband. It is only because he happens to be down with a bout of malaria that she is now holding it openly, though apparently giving less attention to it than to the dazzle beyond the verandah. From her seat she can see a slice of the compound's bare earth, the rickety boundary fence and the path beyond, all framed by exotic orchids and by the large dangling bones of dead animals from which these parasitic plants derive nourishment. She doesn't really see any of it. She's as oblivious of the arrival of her husband's boy as she is of the uncomfortable chair and the ghastly heat, living a fantasy version of what her life would have been if her mother had not married her off at the first opportunity.

Recalling a phrase in the letter, she wonders whether the woman's determination to force her into this particular marriage had anything to do with the name ' white man's grave ' sensationally applied to the region, from which mosquitoes and other disease-carriers have not yet been eliminated. Deciding that the intention probably is that she shall not return, she accepts this without any special feeling, accustomed all her life to being unwanted among people blind to her gifts. It's only at school that her intelligence has ever been recognized; and that period, not many months ago, already seems immeasurably remote — almost mythical — so that she doesn't consider seriously the letter's suggestion. It's as much as she can do to cope with each day as it comes, each one a little hotter than the one before. Unaware of the hostile gaze fixed upon her, she lies dreaming about university life, incapable of the effort of self-assertion that might turn the dream into reality.

Mohammed Dirwaza Khan has ready a question about tonight's dinner (justified by his master's being in bed, and her frequent absences from the meal), should she look up and ask what he wants. He can't understand why she doesn't do so, and suspects her of pretending not to know he is there. The letter is his main interest : like every letter that comes to the house, he has marked its arrival, and noted it in his mind. Her preoccupation with it strikes him as highly significant, and from the care with which she keeps it hidden he has concluded that it is a love letter. He has actually had it in his hands and examined it with the closest attention, but to no purpose, as he can't read English. He daren't take it away to get it translated, sure she will notice if he abstracts it from its hiding place. Looking like an Old Testament prophet with his stern ascetic face and grey beard, he frowns at her disapprovingly; then, deciding nothing is to be gained by watching her any longer, he retires into the house.

Reappearing almost immediately on the back porch, he stares down with a vicious sneer on his face at the recumbent chuprassi, who's sound asleep, his beard stirring slightly each time he breathes out with a little snore. The other man stands poised like a stork on his left leg; the right leg, thin as a stick but immensely strong, shoots out with the sudden force of a mule's, kicking him in the kidneys.

'Pig-dog! Is this how you guard the master's property?' His voice rises to a thin scream.

The chuprassi wakes with a yell of pain, scrambling on all fours, endeavouring at the same time to retrieve his badge of office and to massage the injured spot, pouring out a guttural flood of confused excuses, apologies. The only answer is a violently ejected, neatly aimed blob of spit, which sizzles into the soft dust, making a deep pit there, only just missing his hand.

Having thus aroused his subordinate to a sense of duty Mohammed moves on, his large horny feet with their widely splayed, almost prehensile toes rising and falling soundlessly, impervious to stones, splinters, cactus spines, scorpions, snakes — all the assorted hazards of the compound.

Silently circling the silent house, he rather resembles

an animated, gnarled, ancient piece of wood, from which all sap has long ago been extracted by the relentless sun, padding along, indefatigible, indestructible-seeming, in the blasting noonday heat, watching everything out of unblinking eyes.

## 10

Down the stairs comes a handsome major of about forty, immaculate in R.A.M.C. tropical uniform. The girl is waiting for him at the bottom. She is relieved that his visit has gone off quietly, with no explosions of bad temper on the part of the patient. It now only remains for her to show this army doctor out to his car, waiting in the shade of the porch. She's never met him before, and, as he comes down, looking cool, smart, and assured, he seems to personify all that's acceptable socially, and that she is not. For this reason, his presence makes her slightly uneasy, and she'll be glad when he's gone.

'Not to worry,' he tells her. 'He'll be over this in three or four days.'

His voice is pleasant, but off-hand. She expects him to go straight out to his car, and is surprised when he pauses instead, looking at her. At the same moment, she hears bottles being put down behind her, looks round, and sees that Mohammed Dirwaza Khan has brought a tray of drinks into the sitting-room. The Moslem lifts his head, confronting her with the frown of disapproval he puts on these days when he thinks she's done something wrong, hardly troubling to hide his contempt, now that he's in triumphant charge of the sickroom. The faint flush that appears on her cheeks could equally well be because she's ashamed of not standing up to him, or afraid the major will notice she doesn't, or because it hasn't occurred to her to offer him a drink.

Now she does so, and he accepts. Together they go into the room, which, except for a few books lying about, is just as it was when she saw it for the first time, months ago, and was discouraged, once and for all, by the hopeless dull dreariness of it, which seems beyond improvement. The man isn't interested in the room. It's her youth that has caught his attention — she looks, and is, years younger than most of his women friends — and he fixes his eyes on her while she awkwardly measures whisky into a glass.

They haven't met because she seldom goes to the club, where he is a prominent figure, as he is everywhere, a leading light of the little community, yet, as an army man, above it; a member of a privileged caste. He is universally popular, and has the reputation of being a discreet Don Juan. The men like and admire him; the women are crazy about him.

The girl hands him his glass, suggesting that he add the soda himself. Without taking his eyes off her he squirts the siphon once, then picks up the glass, gazing at her all the time. ' Cheers! ' He lifts it slightly, and drinks. ' Aren't you drinking? '

She shakes her head, her hair swings forward, and she puts it back from her face, rather embarrassed by his prolonged, cool, perfectly open stare. His next remark, too, is embarrassing.

' I've heard a lot about you.' Disregarding her silence, he calmly continues to stare at her without the least concealment, divesting her of her dress . . . is she wearing anything underneath it? No brassière, certainly . . . figure all right without . . . Probably no pants either . . .

She has heard rumours about him, and gives him a

dubious glance. In spite of his good looks she doesn't see him as a romantic figure; to her, he seems middle-aged. She vaguely supposes he's a contemporary of her dead father's, which somehow seems reassuring. Suddenly more at ease, she smiles and tells him: ' I'm sure you haven't heard anything nice about me '. Half aware that she hasn't smiled for a long time, she's grateful to him for making it possible for her to be amused and to speak naturally.

He smiles back, having reached a mainly favourable conclusion about her, though with reservations. Her smile, at least, has charm. Otherwise, he finds her devoid of this quality, like a schoolgirl, with her clumsily-bobbed hair, which must have been cut by one of the local Jap barbers, though it might have been hacked off with nail scissors in the school dorm. He thinks this a pity, since her hair attracts him, and he wants to stroke it. Thick and shining, it's so fine that it stirs all the time in the draught of the fan as if it had life of its own. She herself, on the other hand, strikes him as oddly lifeless, so absent and vague she might almost be sleep-walking. There must be something wrong with her, he can't make it out. She doesn't appear to appreciate the fact that he's sacrificing his valuable time in order to get to know her. How can she be oblivious of this honour? Is it possible that she doesn't realize other women would give their ears to be in her place?

To her surprise, he now asks, ' How are *you*, by the way? ' introducing a personal note via his profession, as she gives him no opening. ' I don't mean to be uncomplementary, but you're looking a bit washed-out — climate getting you down? '

But this gets him nowhere. She misses the point, not

catching on at all, and merely replies : ' I can't get used to this heat '.

' We can't do much about that, I'm afraid.' He begins to sound slightly impatient. ' But cheer up! The rains are coming.'

For a moment they look at one another in silence, the man smiling with automatic charm, giving her a last chance. She feels, but does not understand his dissatisfaction, which only bewilders her, so that she doesn't know what to say to him.

Irritated by such unresponsiveness, his impulse towards her expiring, he gives her up, finally, as a bad job. ' Oh, well, let me know if you feel out of sorts,' he says, not quite hiding his annoyance. He puts down his empty glass and strides to the door, where Mohammed Dirwaza Khan has already appeared, preparatory to seeing him off. The girl stays where she is, calling goodbye to the major, who suddenly seems in a hurry. Exasperated because he's been wasting his time he jumps into his car without answering, accelerates, and is gone.

She is left with that peculiar sense of frustration which results from the unexplained, premature ending of something pleasant. The true cause of the man's behaviour never dawns upon her. He was nice at first; they seemed to be getting on well. So what happened? What did she do wrong?

All at once she starts violently, amazed to see her husband appear. He seems to have grown taller and thinner in bed, and looks an eight-foot skeleton. Even in his pyjamas, which hang loose on his bony frame, he has a sort of overbearing dominance that's rather impressive, although he has to clutch at the furniture for support. She moves instinctively to help him, but stops at the sound of his angry voice.

' Has that bloody pill-merchant gone at last? What have you been doing with him all this time? ' He glares at her out of eyes that seem sunk into his head.

' I only gave him a drink.'

' Drink? ' He seizes upon the word with avid suspicion, accusing her with those eyes, burning with fever in their black cavities.

Dumb and motionless, she watches him slowly work his way into the room, grabbing one chair after another, until he reaches the tray of drinks. Here he holds the whisky bottle up to the light to see how much has gone, next turning his attention to the two glasses, only one of which has been used. This doesn't deter him from examining the other minutely, and even smelling it before putting it down. ' So you haven't taken to the bottle so far,' he says in a nasty tone.

' You know I hate the stuff,' she replies, and adds diffidently : ' Won't you go back to bed? '

He ignores this, looking all round the room with a crafty, suspicious air, as if the major might be hiding behind the furniture. Heaven only knows what makes him see the place objectively for once, in all its impersonal, dreary bareness, just as he took it over from his bachelor predecessor. Dimly recalling his mother's drawing-room, full of chintz and silver rose bowls, he asks the girl : ' Why the hell don't you do something about this room? '

But when she says, ' What? ' he is stumped, unable to fix his elusive dissatisfaction in words, and merely looks around irritably, until he suddenly asks : ' Why aren't there any flowers? '

She couldn't be more astonished if he'd said elephants, bewildered, as she already is, by his sudden unlikely interest. She too looks round the room, with a helpless feeling: it still seems beyond improvement — where could one possibly start?

'Tell the mali to bring some flowers in — buy them in the bazaar if he can't grow them. What do I pay him for?' The man keeps his eyes fixed on her angrily, all his grievances boiling up inside him. He doesn't realize the dismay at the prospect of having another antagonistic native to deal with prevents her from answering; to him, her silence appears a deliberate provocation. It's precisely this silence of hers that he always finds so maddening, and the way she simply sits about doing nothing at all. 'I believe you're trying to drive me insane!' he explodes, at the end of his tether. 'Why don't you ever *do* anything? It's your job to make the house look decent — I thought you were supposed to be so artistic . . .'

The sneer neither relieves his anger nor stops the fever rising in him. Everything is slowly starting to move round and round in the dark closed world that confines him; and, although he clings on tight to the back of a chair, he seems to be floating round too. He longs for the security of his bed, but daren't let go of the chair; in fact, the effort of coming down here has taken so much out of him that he can't move.

It's all his wife's fault. As always, he blames her for everything. If he could trust her he wouldn't have to get up and wander about the house. How dare she bring that devil of a doctor into his home? The whole world seems to be in a conspiracy against him in his illness. And he's helpless. He can only cling on desperately to the chair that looks bloodstained, made of the raw red sticky wood they use in the jail. Even the fan is against him and has started to squeak as it trundles round, making a fiendish sound which strikes right on the nerves, expressly in order to torment him . . . as she does . . . knowing the secret of some sore spot in the depths of his being . . .

The throbbing in his head impels him to brandish his fist — at the fan . . . at the girl . . at the whole bloody universe. In his rage and resentment he can only mumble inconsecutive phrases that fall from his lips like moribund toads. ' — call in that fucking bastard behind my back . . .' And then, shifting to a different grievance : ' To look at this room no one would think a woman lived here . . . it doesn't look like a home at all . . .'

These last words have the totally unforeseen effect of touching off some illumination in the hearer's mind. With sudden hope, she realizes that she's never felt any sense of permanence here; never thought of the place as her home. Which seems to mean that she won't be here for the rest of her life, after all. But she at once loses sight of this gleam of encouragement, as the aggrieved mutterings continue.

The man is so full of rage that he lumps everything into one colossal grievance : the depressing room, the diabolical major, the badly functioning contraption of metal fins on the ceiling, the perfidious wife who's dragged him down here from the sick bed where he ought to be lying — where she ought to be cherishing him, waiting on him . . .

There's nothing left in him now but the sort of blind fury and grievance a bull might feel, pricked by all those maddening banderillas it can't see, stuck in its flesh, from which blood is streaming. Only it's darkness, black blood, that streams into the room, flooding everywhere, so that he's drowning in it. He can't see properly and tries to call for more light, but now he can't get out a word. In front of his eyes his wife's face turns into a pallid clock face, solemnly ticking. He feels he is dying of thirst, his throat and mouth dry as sand. The whisky bottle appears before him, three times larger than life; but when he reaches out for it his arm breaks off at the shoulder.

The throbbing in his head becomes a loud sustained buzz, like a dentist's drill, pierced intermittently by the thin intolerable screech of the fan . . . of a nail hammered through his skull. Everything is rushing away from him, falling apart. Fragmentary elements of a room race past, dissolving in the general torrent of disintegration . . . into which he falls too, and is falling to pieces . . .

Nothing is real any longer; except a pair of thin, blackish, wiry arms, which materialize mysteriously, and mysteriously retain their solidity, grasping him strongly, holding him up . . . and finally carrying him up the stairs like a baby . . .

Luckily for him, he is spared the knowledge of this culminating indignity.

## 11

The mercury in the thermometer by the door has crept up one degree higher this afternoon. Otherwise nothing has altered. The brain-fever birds keep repeating the question that will never be answered. Mr Dog Head is still alternately sweating and shivering, his fever high and his temper vile beyond words. Everything is exactly the same. And yet everything is entirely different, for the girl has a visitor.

The only visitors she's had so far are the condescending club ladies, who occasionally honour her with their presence and patronisingly ask her to join this or that. Now, for the first time, she has a visitor of her very own. And the incredible thing, just like magic, is that this visitor is actually the person she's always wanted to know but been sure she never would, because her husband dislikes all young people. The thought of the sick man makes her feel slightly guilty. But why should she feel guilty? She's not responsible in any way for this amazing meeting, which has come about quite spontaneously, without any action on her part, like a gift from the gods.

She can hardly believe it, and has to keep glancing across to make sure 'the man in suède boots' really is sitting there under the squeaky fan, his legs stuck out in front of him, looking quite at his ease. The famous boots are extremely elegant at close quarters, obviously made for him, in that lovely pale leather, soft and supple as velvet.

The two of them are sedate at first. They talk politely to one another. They sip their tea. They speak of the heat, of the snakes that inhabit the swamp and sometimes crawl on to the path along which the young man walks every day to his work. In serious tones they mention the power of coincidence : if he hadn't killed that snake . . . if she hadn't happened to see him from the verandah . . .

In a sudden flash, she knows that here is someone she really *can* talk to — it's like being released from solitary confinement at last! Her pleasure is so evident that he feels glad too. There really seems to be something rather remarkable about their meeting. The girl is a bit carried away, intoxicated almost, by the wonderful new prospect of communication. The young man has been lonely too, among all those much older chaps who order him about and make fun of his expensive mosquito boots — it says something for his independence that he hasn't been teased out of wearing them. He is relieved now to be with somebody near his own age for a change; somebody who obviously likes him.

He's seen her before at the club, but she's always been quiet — stand-offish, he has assumed, judging her by that awful husband with the notorious temper who thinks he's God Almighty and quarrels with everyone. Now he finds that she's really quite different : engaging and rather quaint, unlike other girls. All of a sudden, he is reminded of the young sister he's fond of, who has the same vague, dreamy, helpless look which appeals to the masculine chivalry inculcated during his schooldays, which he hasn't grown out of yet.

He thinks what a perfect infant she looks — that husband must be a real baby-snatcher. And before he knows it he's asking how she comes to be living out here as a married woman when she looks as if she ought to be still at school. 'Why did you marry a man so much older, and so . . .' He breaks off, not liking to say what's in his mind about the fellow's queer reputation, and certain rumours he's heard . . .

Without any further encouragement, she starts telling him her life story. It's been bottled up inside her so long that it comes pouring out to the first sympathetic listener. 'I never wanted to marry him, or anyone else . . . I was going to the university, I had a scholarship . . . It was my mother who insisted that I should get married instead . . .' She tells him this quite simply, like a good little girl who always obeys the grown-ups because they know best.

'What a damn shame!' He stares at her, a bit staggered — can such things happen in these days?

But she takes it perfectly calmly, as a matter of course. 'You see, my mother wanted to get rid of me. She never liked me — nobody ever does.'

'Well, *I* do!' he asserts promptly.

On the spot she decides he's the nicest person she's ever known, and looks at him gratefully, without speaking. Their eyes meet, and something happens. They both feel slightly overcome without quite knowing why. To extricate them from embarrassment she continues: 'I don't think my husband likes me — he says it's my fault he's gone down with malaria'.

'How could it possibly be your fault?' Reacting from that curious moment just now, Suède Boots bursts out laughing. 'Sorry — but I can't help it! I never heard such rot!'

So it's actually possible to laugh in this house! The breezy infectious sound quite astounds her — she's almost forgotten what laughter's like. He seems to break some spell by laughing, for she finds herself laughing too . . . as long as she doesn't remember about the rats . . .

Now they chatter away like old friends, their heads close together. He's only a year or two older than she is, and, as they're both so very young, a somewhat childish atmosphere builds up around them. The continuous buzz of the fan encloses them in a small tent of sound, a private room of their own where they're oblivious of the passing of time.

The three windows behind them, on the shady side of the house, are wide open. They are deep in their conversation. Neither of them notices, or looks round, when, framed by the first window, a big white turban appears, surmounting a bearded face which gazes in and then vanishes, reappearing at the second window, where it stays rather longer. At the third window it does not put in an appearance, presumably having already seen all there is to see — which certainly isn't much.

Soon after this Suède Boots looks at his watch. ' Heavens! I must be going! ' He pushes back his chair, but seems stuck to it. He doesn't want to leave her. They start talking again. But he thinks of the husband in bed upstairs and feels slightly uneasy. Does the man know he is here? If so, he must be wondering what on earth they are talking about all this time. ' I really must get along now.' He stands up, suddenly determined, says goodbye to her briskly, and walks off, pushing between the panels of the door.

To the girl, it's as if he takes the light with him.

She listens to his receding steps, which sound rather loud on the stone floor. For some reason this makes her think of the man upstairs too. But what does it matter if he hears? There's nothing he can object to in someone coming to tea — what could be more harmless? Nevertheless, she suddenly feels alarmed. She can't let her visitor go like this, and runs after him impulsively, catching him on the verandah just as he's about to step down to the compound.

'Hello!' he says, surprised to see her. He doesn't want to delay his departure, having got to this point. Besides, this is no place for lingering over goodbyes; although the porch cuts off the full impact of the afternoon heat and glare it's far too hot to be comfortable.

She feels his impatience, almost feeling he's lost already. Instead of looking at him she looks down at the splintery wood under her feet as she asks, in a whisper almost: 'Shall I see you again?' hanging her head and hiding behind her hair.

'Of course. Tomorrow — why not?' he replies, so positively that at first she feels better. But after a moment he seems to be tempting providence by being so certain. Her fears return, and she murmurs pathetically:

'Everything always goes wrong with me . . .' On her face is the helplessly apprehensive look of a child who knows the grown-ups will disapprove of her new friend and forbid them to meet again; and, like a child, she feels this will be the end of the world — she can't see past such a disaster.

But as he doesn't know what is in her mind her behaviour seems a bit odd, artificial; he thinks she's pretending to be a sort of 'tragedy queen' to impress him. All the same he assures her that, where he is concerned, everything about her is quite all right.

Grateful, she gives him her attractive smile. And, because she really seems rather a sweet child, even if she does make a drama out of nothing, he recklessly tells her he'll drop in each day, as he has to pass anyhow, until she gets tired of him and tells him not to. He smiles again, waves his hand in final farewell, jumps the three steps to the compound and hurries out of her sight.

Instead of going back to the room with the fan, where it's cooler, she stays there, staring after him, still feeling a little disturbed without admitting the reason. A big lizard, hidden in the rafters over her head, starts tonelessly repeating, Gekko, gekko, gekko, like a clock striking. While simultaneously, giving her a fright, Mohammed Dirwaza Khan unexpectedly appears, his big bare feet soundless on the steps from the compound. With bent head he quickly slips past, no expression whatever on his averted face.

All her obscure alarms are strengthened, alarming questions come into her head, one after another. What was he doing out there in the sun, at this time, when he's supposed to be off duty? Why did he come in this way, when he never uses the front entrance? Why didn't he look at her?

She runs down the steps and stands at the extreme edge of the porch's shadow, looking all round, her eyes searching the searing dazzle outside. Suède Boots has vanished already. The compound is deserted, the road and the pathway too. Nobody is to be seen anywhere. Nothing is happening.

It's too hot to stay here, and she turns back to the

house. The lizard is still calling, Gekko, as she goes in. She counts its cries mechanically. There are twelve more of them.

## 12

Suède Boots is here again for tea. He looks in every day as he promised, and fancies he's falling a little in love with the girl, though not seriously enough to commit himself. Now and then, when he remembers his existence, he's faintly worried about the husband, who has recovered and is now back at work. He hears that he hasn't once mentioned him, and wonders whether he doesn't know about his daily visits. But that's impossible in this grapevine country, where each branch sprouts a crop of wide open ears — how extraordinary that he makes no comment. He tells himself the man must be simply indifferent, or perhaps even glad to have someone talk to his wife, so that he needn't bother. But as he never has bothered about her in the slightest the argument is not very convincing.

Marvellous to relate, nobody seems to have noticed his visits. And as few Europeans use the marsh path he deludes himself into believing they can escape observation indefinitely. Of course he's not ashamed of going to see the girl — quite the reverse. But he knows, once the secret is out, the two of them are bound to become targets for pernicious gossip; their innocent relationship will be smeared with all sorts of disgusting hints and rumours. In this climate, always seething with sex, the small white community is a hotbed of scandal. An intense interest is taken in each new affair that comes to light, which is endlessly discussed and reported, without much regard for truth. Some people, with too little to do and over-stimulated by the heat, seem to confuse reality with the sexual fantasies they embellish with obscene detail, and are apt to accuse others of indulging in their own perverse imaginings. He knows how hungrily they will pounce on the news, circulating it eagerly among themselves, distorted out of all recognition by their morbid fancies. He hates to think of his pure affection being so basely degraded, and can't bear the idea of the girl being victimized either, as she's so helpless and vulnerable.

However, his youthful optimism prevents him from being seriously troubled. He concentrates on enjoying the present, without too much concern for future eventualities. Things are going very well at the moment; the girl seems happier and more relaxed — when he's with her, at any rate. Not being insensitive, he has become aware of her idea that she's doomed to perpetual bad luck, but feels sure he'll be able to make her outlook more cheerful.

For a start, he's already almost persuaded her that their friendship will be allowed to go on. If only he could spend more time with her. His visits are always far too short for all they have to talk about. They discuss everything under the sun, and also laugh a good deal — she has so much lost laughter to make up for. But this afternoon, as it happens, the conversation is more serious, for she's just told him about the precious letter, and brought it downstairs to show him.

When the bearded spy, unsuspected, unseen, for a moment looks in at the window, he's puzzled by the sight of their two heads bent over the familiar worn sheet of notepaper, which doesn't seem to fit in very well with his love-letter theory.

In blissful ignorance of him and his machinations, Suède Boots tells her it certainly isn't too late to do as the letter writer suggests, and take up her scholarship at the university. Why should she stay out here, in this vile climate, tied to a man twice her age she ought never to have married, who neglects her, and whom she doesn't care twopence about? He gets quite excited while he is talking, and is disappointed because at the end she says nothing. Her face is half hidden from him by her hair, which falls forward as she bends over the letter, carefully returning it to its envelope.

He always likes to look at her hair. She must have washed it today, as it is slightly ruffled and there seems more of it than usual. The straight, fair hair refuses to conform to the shape in which it's been clumsily cut, and strands keep on escaping. The fan stirs individual hairs on the surface, and their tiny movements, amplified by the mass of hair, create constantly changing eddies with shining highlights. But, attractive as it is in itself, the hair's perpetual motion accentuates its owner's unmoving silence, which begins to make him slightly impatient. He can't understand why she puts up with the situation, without even trying to change it, which he thinks she could easily do.

' All you've got to do is walk out and book your passage,' he tells her: and, as she still doesn't speak, adds impatiently: ' You're not in prison! ' Still he waits in vain for her to say something, and finally bursts out: ' You've only got one life, you know! Are you always going to let other people run it for you, as if you were six years old? '

Even now she can't think of an answer. She knows that however often he repeats that it's quite easy for her to get on a boat or a plane, the proposition will remain purely theoretical to her; it will never, for a single instant, appear as something she might actually *do*. She looks at him appealingly, as if to beg him not to be angry with her. She doesn't want to annoy him, but feels incapable of explaining how impossible it is for her to resume her old life where it was broken off. She'll never make him understand that an impassable barrier separates her from her past — for him, impassable barriers don't exist. The only thing seems to be to put forward the obvious obstacle of having no money.

And this he immediately sweeps aside with the greatest of ease, disposing of it at once. He will pay her fare for her. She can pay him back any time. Or never. It doesn't matter. His parents are rich, it appears, and have only sent him out here for a year or so to toughen him up, and because of certain youthful escapades he refers to with a wry grimace, without going into details.

At last she now lifts her head, putting back her hair with one hand, and wonderingly looks him full in the face. No one has ever treated her generously before; she is touched and astonished by his generosity. She can't bear to seem ungrateful, and hasn't the heart to refuse his offer, although the project seems just as unreal as it did before. To please him, she promises to think it over, and meanwhile continues to look at him — her expression almost makes him get up and hug her.

Instead, he changes the subject, reverting to one they've already discussed several times, which involves a question nearly as difficult for her to answer. He wants to take her out in his car for a picnic; they can drive down to the river, where there's generally a cool breeze, or go a little way into the jungle she's never seen. There's nothing in the world she'd like better. Yet whenever he asks her to fix a day she always becomes evasive and puts him off, in spite of the fact that they could easily get back before her husband, who often works late at his office. He can't understand it — he would never guess her real reason in a thousand years.

It is that she has a superstitious desire to keep everything the same between them. Any innovation seems dangerous, a threat to her precarious present happiness. If it were possible, she'd like to go on forever re-living that first afternoon, having the same identical conversation ad infinitum. Though she won't admit it, at the back of her mind is a constant dread of some fatal nightmare moment when everything will have to stop. But this fear is too formless and too obscure to put into words, so she never mentions it to him.

' We'll have to go very soon, if we're ever going,' he now remarks, with fresh urgency. ' It's impossible to go anywhere once the rains break.'

With passing surprise, she perceives that even the frightful heat has become unimportant to her lately. But now that she thinks of the weather she feels the added oppressiveness in the air and a new undercurrent of tension, like electricity — almost like something about to explode. She's still searching for a reply that won't displease him when, to her relief, a brain-fever bird in the tamarinds calls out so loudly that she can't be expected to say anything till it stops.

Who-are-you? Who-are-you? Who-are-you? echoes

another bird, in flight seemingly, the question getting louder and louder as it approaches; it flaps and flutters among the green clusters of the banana trees just outside, shouts, Who-are-you? right into the room, then flies off again, still calling out at the top of its voice the question nobody ever answers, which is repeated by all the other brain-fever birds for miles around.

Who-are-you? Who-are-you? Who-are-you? The mounting volume of noise comes from both sides of the house, from the back, from the front, from the compound, the road, the swamp, the trees, from everywhere at once. Hundreds, thousands of birds are all shouting their heads off — the girl's never heard them make such a racket. The frantic cries sound to her not only demented but threatening, so that she feels uneasy. Some of them seem to sound distinctly ominous. Yet she must imagine this, for, in reality, all the cries are exactly alike. All have the same infuriating, monotonous, unstoppable persistence; all sound equally mechanical, motiveless, not expressing anger, or fear, or love, or any sort of avian feeling — their sole function seems to be to drive people mad.

No human voice can compete with the din. The two under the fan have to sit helplessly, waiting for the row to subside. Suède Boots smiles, and she, disguising the uneasiness she can't get rid of, smiles back. Her hands have instinctively covered her ears, but she lowers them with the intention of asking if all the birds have gone suddenly crazy. At the same moment, however, she notices that he is no longer smiling.

He has already heard the new sound she is only just catching, which is also mechanical and monotonous and has the same inexorable persistence common to all machine-made noise, that goes on and on, indifferent to everything. It's not easy to follow the low hum, or rumble, through the delirious pandemonium of the birds' repetitive questions. Hardly has she recognized it as the sound of an approaching car than it stops suddenly.

Everything stops with it. Or so it seems. The birds' cries, at any rate, are abruptly cut off, and it's impossible to tell whether they've been interrupted by the car, or whether their explosive outburst has come to its natural conclusion. In the sudden silence, the footsteps which can be heard steadily coming nearer sound unnaturally loud. Beating on the stone floor with the terrifying, inflexible regularity of a machine nobody can stop, they progress towards the door, the flaps of which fly apart to admit Mr Dog Head.

He stands a few paces away, staring at the pair. His cold, very bright blue eyes have a glint that seems not quite normal. His hat has left a red ring round his forehead; it might be the diadem of a prince to judge by his haughty, domineering expression. No one speaks or moves. All three of them seem held in suspense, as if mesmerized. Only the fan continues its lackadaisical circling, the high squeak it emits with each revolution now piercingly loud.

This of course is the moment the girl dreads, when everything will suddenly come to an end. Although her fear isn't fully conscious she feels she must make some kind of effort to save her happiness. She starts moving the teapot in front of her as if it were some heavy object, but doesn't manage to complete the gesture, which would be futile in any case. 'Will you have some tea?' Her low voice travels a little way into the silence, but seems to make no headway against it, and expires, leaving her mute and motionless as before.

Her husband takes no notice whatever of her. His blue eyes stare icily, fixedly, at the visitor, with disgust and abysmal contempt. His big aristocratic nose arches itself superciliously as he asks, ' What are *you* doing here? ' as though he were asking : ' Why did *you* ever have to emerge from the primordial slime? '

Suède Boots, who's got up in confusion, stammers something, steps forward and holds out his hand, hardly knowing what he is doing — the man's lordly, insulting behaviour, combined with the tension it's impossible to ignore, deprive him completely of his usual aplomb.

For a second, or for several seconds, these two confront one another. They are dressed alike. Both wear shorts, and a short-sleeved bush jacket which, with belt, numerous buttoned pockets and shoulder tabs has a vaguely military aspect. But while in one case this might be the uniform of a general, in the other it's more like a Boy Scout's. The wearer's young, bare, rounded knees look half pathetic, half comic; most unlike the tough, sinewy, hairy knees of his much taller senior, who is in every way far more formidable, in his arrogance and his gaunt, mature, muscular virility, beneath which can be felt a disturbing suggestion of something faintly unbalanced.

Suddenly, without warning, in sudden mad irritability, Dog Head lifts his clenched fist and brings it down with terrific force on the outstretched hand, knocking it away from him. ' Out! ' he snaps, like a savage dog; the single-syllable command, and the accompanying jerk of the head, both express ultimate scorn.

The young man goes very red in the face, and,

inarticulate with pain and rage, bursts into unintelligible indignation, looking more than ever like a furious little boy, almost on the verge of tears. He's like a sort of juvenile Jack the Giant Killer before his opponent. Except that it's obviously the giant who will do the killing in this case.

' Out ! ' The command is snapped for the second time, with insufferable superiority. ' Or are you waiting to be slung out by the scruff of your neck? '

The young fellow's red face turns quite pale now, but he gamely assumes a fighting attitude, although it's only too evident to him that he hasn't a chance — not a hope in hell — against this lunatic, who will ' wipe the floor with him ', ' make mincemeat of him ', etc.

But at the last moment, the girl saves the situation for him by crying, ' Oh, no . . ! ' and hiding her face in her hands.

Whereupon, much relieved, he sensibly abandons his pugilistic stance, thankful for the chance to retire without being branded a coward. He pretends he is doing it for her sake, as he hurries out of the room, avoiding her with his eyes, and looking extremely uncomfortable as well as shamefaced.

As if materialized by the order, ' Go and make sure he is off the premises,' Mohammed Dirwaza Khan receives the command with a bow, and immediately glides out in silent pursuit of the departing guest.

Husband and wife are now left alone. The latter hasn't moved, and remains in the same position, her face hidden, while the fan's squeak reaches a maddening climax, rasping the nerves. Owing to the defective mechanism, the high, shrill screech is repeated at slightly irregular intervals, and these marginal variations are unpredictable, and as agonizing as Chinese water torture.

The girl's silence is unendurable to the man, who now comes forward and stops in front of her, his eyes flaring crazily. As she still doesn't speak or look up, he seizes her shoulders, and roughly shakes her backwards and forwards to force her to attend to him.

'Are you listening to me?'— even now he's not certain — 'That piddling pup isn't to come into this house again — ever! Do you understand?'

Even this doesn't make her open her mouth. And when, after a minute, he lets her go, she at once returns to her former pose, with her face in her hands. The only difference is that his rough handling has further disarranged the untidy hair, which now falls over her hands and wrists in such a way as to leave the back of her neck uncovered. More of the pale shiny mass of hair is exposed to the draught of the fan, loose strands of it thrust themselves out like tentacles in different directions, the many separate hairs on the surface weave in and out of each other continually, producing unexpected tremors and eddies, surrounding her bowed head with a misty effect, as ceaselessly circling insects surround a lamp.

The man is in a black rage, scowling, and compressing his lips till they disappear in a thin line, clenching and unclenching his hands convulsively. Convinced she's deliberately taunting him, he takes her silence as a challenge to his inborn supremacy, which is intolerable. Nor can he endure this frustration — why can't he *make* her speak?

As he stands there, looking down at her, baffled, very slowly a faint tinge of doubt invades his furious, overbearing expression. He has no idea what to do next.

The quinine, already buzzing inside his head, blends with the squeal of the fan in a fiendish disharmony, increasing his rage and frustration to an insufferable degree of intensity. The lightly stirring hairs he is staring at seem to dissolve in mist . . . through which all he sees is the nape of her neck, pale and sprinkled all over with small, faintly glistening beads, stretched out before him like that of a victim waiting for execution . . .

Such a murderous frenzy of violence surges through him that, shocked by it, he turns away blindly, and hurries out of the room.

## 13

As soon as the Suède Boots episode ends, it seems never to have happened. It's almost as though there has never been any such person, as he no longer passes the house, preferring to make a lengthy detour, that must waste a lot of his time.

Dog Head has satisfactorily intimidated *him*. It's his wife he doesn't seem able to master. She never even says she's sorry — not a word of apology does she utter. He doesn't suspect her of a serious affair, but imagines people are laughing at him, which makes him mad. It's outrageous that she should dare to humiliate him like this. Somehow he simply must get his own back.

Officially the subject is closed. He doesn't refer to it any more. All goes on as before. But, though outwardly he is the same as ever, underneath he seems to be changing. Always now there's that indefinable hint about him of something queer, almost like a touch of madness. A mad frenzy of resentment against her has got into him, which increases as the days pass. The atmosphere is changing too, in the house and outside. Every day the heat grows more intolerable; a weird undercurrent of electrical tension builds up . . . an uncanny excitement . . . as in a dream that has moved imperceptibly into nightmare . . .

He doesn't want to be with his wife, everything about her gets on his nerves, and yet he can't leave her alone. If he asks her to ride or play tennis with him, she always refuses. It exasperates him beyond words to see her mooning about aimlessly, or sitting for hours with her nose stuck in a book. If she's too lazy to take healthy exercise, he asks why she doesn't at least talk to the other women.

She knows it's foolish to answer such questions but, her nerves not being immune to the general tension, is provoked into saying: 'What can I talk about? If I mention anything that interests me, a book or a play, they think I'm affected — they don't understand intelligent conversation.'

This brings forth: 'Fuck you and your intelligent conversation!' The man looks at her in blazing indignation; how dare she put on airs just because she's supposed to be brainy? His arrogant face frightens her, the blue flame in his eyes really does seem a little mad, and she avoids him as much as she can.

Periodically his work takes him away for a day or two, which ought to be a relief. But then her absolute loneliness falls on her like a ton weight. The house is silent, full of heat, emptiness, and the hostility of the servants, who watch her with black unfriendly eyes as she eats her solitary meals. If only she could have her food on a tray somewhere! But of course that's not to be thought of. The household routine must go on. Everything has been settled for her in advance by people who don't wish her well. Why are they all against her? She remembers the women who used to say, 'You'll get to like living here in time,' their voices showing they knew very well that she *wouldn't* like it, and were gloating over the fact.

What on earth is she doing here, anyway, among all these brain-fever birds, parrots, vultures, snakes, scorpions, big bright spiders, and ants that can eat a whole bush in half an hour? It doesn't seem to be her life at all. It's more like a dream, that only is not a nightmare because she knows it won't last for ever — this is the knowledge that keeps her going.

In the meantime, the days seem endless. Each day is like a balloon, blown up to bursting point by the heat and the tension of the approaching monsoon. Electric tension gathers beneath the great clouds that pile up — always gone the next morning — while the earth swelters in airless suspense. It's too hot to think, even. She seems to spend her time waiting — for night to come, or simply for the next minute.

She drags herself up the stairs to put some eau-de-Cologne on her neck and forehead, and afterwards wanders out on to the flat roof of the porch. Out here it seems hotter than ever, in the unnatural half-light under the clouds. She's never seen such clouds, enormous, massive, menacing, black, with yellow underbellies, forming an iron roof over the simmering world. Their shadow brings a strange burning hush in which a gong booms out startlingly. And suddenly a single tremendous buffet of hot wind, like a blast from the devil's furnace, almost sweeps her off her feet, showering her with dust and the small, dry, shrivelled leaves of the tamarinds.

Her eyes are still full of dust, she hasn't had time to collect herself, when the youth who wears the white turban appears behind her. 'Missis come in now,' he orders disapprovingly, his attitude towards her modeled on that of his superior.

As she steps inside he immediately slams the shutters, and then goes all round the house, banging them to with a noise of protest. Padding away finally on his bare feet, he leaves her to stew in solitude under the squeaky fan, in the simmering gloom that seems like the end of the world.

It's too dark to read, and, when she switches the light on, the heat of the bulb slaps her face. So she turns it out again, kicks off her sandals, and sits doing nothing, simply waiting for time to pass, abandoned to heat and discomfort. Presently she hears someone coming, and rouses herself from this daze; her feet instinctively find their way back into the discarded sandals.

In comes Mr Dog Head, sweat streaming down his face, but otherwise unaffected by the heat, which he won't condescend to notice. Forgetting the nightmarish atmosphere momentarily, the girl actually finds his arrival a welcome break in the arid, interminable, eventless expanse of time. She smiles and says, ' Hello,' blinking in the daylight that streams into the room after him, against which he stands outlined. How can he be so impervious to the heat?—it doesn't seem human. His tough, angular frame might be made of metal, or any substance that isn't sensitive to the temperature.

' Sitting in the dark? ' He neither smiles nor returns her greeting, addressing her in the same disapproving tone that the servant used not long ago. Even before she hears his censorious voice and sees him eyeing her with suspicion, she recalls despairingly the hopelessness of attempting to talk to him. And she says no more.

As he hasn't seen her for a few days he looks at her more attentively than usual, noticing that she's become paler and thinner than she used to be; which she seems to have done on purpose to annoy him, so that he snaps : ' What's the matter with you? Aren't you well? '

She can't see his face clearly against the light, but

doesn't need to, being only too familiar with that particular overbearing tone — surely he isn't going to start
a quarrel already? She feels she can't stand the effort of
quarrelling in this appalling heat, and says quietly that
the weather makes her head ache.

'You strain your eyes reading too much,' he retorts.
Then : ' Why the devil can't you get used to the climate,
like everyone else? ' Her failure to make this adjustment
also seems an exasperating device for making him
angry. But, though she doesn't answer, he lets it go,
preoccupied with a new idea, originating in her looking
unwell, which slowly takes shape in his head.

The way he's still staring reminds her that she hasn't
tidied her hair since the wind blew it about, and she
smoothes it down with her hands, so that it catches his
eye. He looks at the glossy, vigorous hair, in which all
her vitality seems concentrated, and which is now so long
that it rests on her shoulders, as she hasn't had the
energy lately even to have it cut. All at once, he finds
that his hands are twitching involuntarily — he wants to
stroke it, which he hasn't done since the period of his
infatuation. His gaze becoming proprietory, possessive,
he takes a sudden step forward and puts his hand on her
shoulder.

She is quite unprepared for this, thinking only about
her hair. It makes her jump to feel the big, hard, heavy
hand descend on her shoulder, like a policeman's, and
tighten its grip there.

' Anything happened while I've been away? ' he asks
now, in a changed, peculiar tone, ingratiating and
artificial; he doesn't really want to know, or expect an
answer, and might equally well have made any other
remark. The question is in the nature of a preliminary,

part of a routine, which she recognizes with horror from the bedroom, as he pulls her against him.

She feels the insufferable heat generated between their two touching bodies spring up like a flame and, acting purely on impulse, not stopping to think, wrenches herself out of his grasp. Instantly a murderous flare appears in his blue eyes, his face goes rigid, his hands clench as if to drag out by the roots handfuls of the hair they were about to caress. But he says nothing, turning his back on her, and marches out of the room.

She doesn't see him again until they meet at dinner, when he hardly speaks a word. To pay her out, as soon as the meal is over, he gets the racquets and starts the rat game. Though he can't compel her to play with him, he forces her to stay in the room. But she shuts her eyes tight and won't watch, so he's frustrated again.

He feels like bashing her with the racquet, and is only restrained by the resolve that's come to him suddenly to make her give him a son and heir; it's the least she can do in return for the honour of being married to him. Besides, it will take her down a peg or two, and show her which of them is the boss.

Grinning to himself over these thoughts, he goes on bashing the rats with particular gusto.

## 14

Without warning one evening, while dinner is being served, the electric light starts to fade. It doesn't go out altogether, but gives the impression of being about to do so at any moment, meanwhile maintaining a rapid, distracting, continuous flickering that has a distorting, hallucinatory effect, and makes everything seem unstable, unreal.

The girl asks what's gone wrong, looking anxiously at her husband. Any mishap of this sort generally starts him swearing and shouting abuse at everyone within earshot. But to her surprise he remains calm and only says, ' It's always like this at the end of the hot weather,' adding something about hydraulic pressure she doesn't take in.

The queer quick fluctuations have already made her disagreeably conscious that her head is aching; also, they produce a disturbing, impossible effect, as if the day's shimmering heat-haze had invaded the night-time room. Which is doubtless why she doesn't notice when, after the butler has handed the main dish, the vegetables are offered, not by his proper assistant, but by the youth in the white turban.

Nor does the man at the head of the table appear to be aware of any irregularity in the service, as he helps himself generously. He keeps his eyes on his plate, eating with his usual appetite, preparing each mouthful in advance, putting it into his mouth and repeating the process before he's finished masticating the last, displaying a somewhat doglike conscientiousness in scrupulously cleaning up every morsel. After he's consumed a second helping with the same thoroughness, and while the butler's occupied with the next course, the youth slips out to the back porch. Here Mohammed Dirwaza Khan is waiting for him and mutters a brief question, which he answers by a quick affirmative nod, returning immediately to the dining-room.

His bearded superior too leaves the porch at once, silent as a shadow, entering the central corridor which divides the house and into which the stairs and all the rooms lead. He passes the flickering light in the dining-room, where only his master's legs are visible under the door flaps, and, without attracting attention or making a sound, mounts to the floor above. He does not hurry. If he is seen, he is merely on his way to prepare his master's room for the night, as he always does at about this time.

Instead, however, he goes straight into the girl's room, which he's never supposed to enter. Considering this fact, he's remarkably well acquainted with its contents and their exact position, for, without putting on the light, guided only by the feeble wavering gleam from below, he goes straight to the cupboard where she keeps her dresses, and a row of shoes on a shelf underneath.

He makes a sign of superstitious significance, to avert whatever evil would otherwise befall him in consequence of touching these forbidden objects, then squats down on his haunches and, with evident aversion, picks up one shoe gingerly, shakes it, and puts it back, picking up the next. In the near-darkness it's hard to see what exactly his gnarled strong fingers are doing as they busy themselves with the shoes; but his activities are certainly not legitimate, though there is nothing furtive about his movements, and only their speed indicates a desire to finish the operation before dinner is over. Picking up each shoe in turn he eventually finds what he's looking for, extracting from the toe of one a sheet of notepaper, folded very small, which has been handled so much that it's practically falling to pieces. This is not the first time he's had it in his possession; but he shows considerable interest in it now, taking it into the lighter centre room, where he stands at the top of the stairs, scrutinizing it closely, turning it this way and that, as if a new angle might make it disclose its secret. He surveys it for some time upside-down before slipping it into his pocket and silently entering his master's room, just as the scraping of chairs below marks the end of the meal.

He stays here, letting down and arranging the mosquito net, and performing several other small duties, as he does every night, until Dog Head comes in calling for his racquet. This he solemnly gets out of a cupboard, dusting the strings and undoing the nuts of the old-fashioned press; while its owner, with his hand inside his shirt, stands waiting, scratching his hairy chest. Nothing is said. No looks are exchanged. It's quite impossible to tell whether the master knows what his servant has just been doing. He shows no surprise when the letter is produced and handed to him, but this he would be unlikely to do before an inferior, in any case.

The Mohammedan makes rather a long statement in his own language, to which he replies, fluently but concisely, and then sends him away, still as if nothing out of the ordinary had occurred. No doubt he is well aware, from his long experience of eastern customs and intrigue, that he's not required to admit complicity with a subordinate, who must be prepared to shoulder the whole of the blame should this be necessary.

It's just as well for the said subordinate that the letter is not read in his presence, for its contents obviously displease the reader, whose muttered curses seem directed against *him* rather than the letter's recipient. Dog Head's hand, backed with sparse reddish hair, clutches the fragile paper as though he were going to crumple it up; but caution or cunning makes him hesitate. Still holding it in his hand, he goes to the door.

He is tall enough to see over the centre panels by stretching his neck slightly, and looks into the next room, where the girl is sitting as usual close to the screened window, with a book in her lap. She appears to be reading, although the dim, unsteady light is so far away from her that this is not possible, unless she has trained herself to read in the dark.

Her husband watches for a few moments, frowning : then glances, undecided, from her to the flimsy piece of notepaper, wondering how to use it against her to the best advantage. Since this doesn't seem to be the right moment, he ends by putting it away in his wallet.

He then picks up the racquet, and makes some practice strokes, powerful forehand and backhand drives, before going in to try and bully her into playing the rat game with him.

## 15

It has now become almost too hot to live. One would think the fiery core of the earth had come to the surface, so that the shallowest excavation would reveal raging flames. The world is assuming a uniform coppery tinge with shades of orange, like a Martian landscape. Each afternoon the giant clouds gather and slowly roof in the world, excitement and tension accumulating beneath. Each morning the sun leaps triumphantly, unchallenged, into an empty sky; but always, by midday, the clouds are back, pitch black and sulphur yellow, inexorably piling up overhead; while the red-hot earth seethes like an immense cauldron in the eerie thunderlight of an eclipse, electric tremors vibrating in the breathless air.

The excitement of the approaching monsoon emanates from the servants, who appear with strange additions to their usual attire — flowers, medallions, and silk head-scarves they twist into points like rabbit's ears. They might be zombies, working in absence, their whole attention concentrated elsewhere, in secret, intense, febrile preoccupation. The girl feels they may vanish at any moment, to go about their own compulsive mysterious affairs.

Gongs boom at all hours of the day and night. More bullock carts than usual pass on the road, in clouds of dust, fluttering flowers and pennants; and sudden weird falsetto singing bursts out, or the unexpected squeal of a pipe. Everybody is waiting, tense. A peculiar coppery film hangs in the upper air, as though electricity were made visible.

'When will the rains come?' she keeps asking wearily: always receiving the same noncommittal reply from her husband: 'Soon.' He always seems to be watching her these days, out of those eyes that look to her like bits of blue glass but which now have a new glint of cunning, a disturbing secretiveness. She gets the uneasy feeling that he's planning something against her in secret, though she can't conceive what it is.

The strain of trying to read by the flickering dim light has given her a permanent headache. But one good thing about the unsteadiness of the light is that it interferes with the rat game. This evening the player gives up after a few unsuccessful slashes, and hurls his racquet into a corner, swearing loudly. A few moments later, she hears the car start and drive away.

Now she's alone in the house. The servants have all gone to their own quarters, and might be on another planet. Night has brought no relief from the heat. Looking out of her window, she's surprised to see the great clouds racing across the sky, though down here the air is as still as death — the effect is rather uncanny. She fancies she can still make out the queer metallic film under the hurrying clouds, except when the moon escapes them for a second, showing a sick livid face which is engulfed again almost immediately.

She slips off the sandals she's been wearing for days — it's far too hot to wear shoes, she hasn't even looked at her shoes lately. Why should she notice, in any case, if they are disarranged? The servants are often careless about putting things in their right places; she's told them dozens of times not to put books upside down in the shelves, and shown them how to tell top from bottom, but still they go on making the same mistake.

Taking off her clothes, she goes into the bathroom and turns on the shower; it reluctantly yields a thin trickle of scalding water, which gradually cools to tepid — supplies are getting low. The water refuses to run cold, and this luke-warm spray only makes her hotter than ever. After it, she can't bear to put on even the thinnest nightdress, but drapes the flimsy garment round her shoulders, and sits on the edge of the bed, too hot to lie down.

The fan in here has also developed a squeak that disturbs her and finds its way into her dreams. She always means to see about getting the fans put right, but hasn't the energy when it comes to the point. She wouldn't be able to sleep in this heat, anyway. Already, directly after her shower, her whole body is burning hot; a rivulet of sweat runs between her shoulder blades, the nightgown sticks uncomfortably to her shoulders. Shrugging it off, she lets the fan play on her naked flesh. The heat is stifling, volcanic, as if masses of lava were pressing against the walls. Her eyes are dry and hot in her aching head; she can't make the effort to read a book, and knows she won't sleep . . . so what can she do? Shutting her eyes, she presses her fingers against the eyeballs, and sits limply under the fan. Without actually thinking about her husband, she's vaguely relieved because he is not in the house.

Perhaps she dozes for a few moments — anyhow, there he is suddenly, in the room, right in front of her. Startled, she snatches the nightdress and covers herself; how can she not have heard the car?

'Why so modest?' he sneers with a vicious leer. And

she knows he's been drinking as usual. There is a dangerous look about him, he looks a bully, a touch of hysteria in his slightly unbalanced air.

The white trousers he put on for dinner are now crumpled, his shirt is undone to the waist, displaying his hairy chest, which he scratches, raking his fingernails through the reddish fur, as he comes towards her, moving his big, muscular, bony body like a machine which can't be stopped or avoided. He is so close to her now that she can smell his male sweat, mixed with the stale smells of smoke and whisky.

'What about this?' he demands suddenly, and, to her utter astonishment, flourishes a sheet of writing paper in front of her face, which she recognizes at once by the heading, exclaiming: 'My letter!' indignantly reaching out for it.

'Oh, no!' jeers the man, snatching it back and stowing it away for future use. 'So you're planning to rat on me, are you, behind my back?' His voice has become venomous; he stands over her menacingly, his lips tightly compressed, a muscle twitching above the jawline, his blue domineering eyes madly bright.

'I'm not planning anything,' she mutters, overcome by shuddering repulsion at the word rat, and shrinking away from him.

'You'd better not!' Suddenly violent, he seizes the flimsy nightdress and, with one savage tug, rips it in half, tossing the pieces over his shoulder. 'Come here!' he shouts, determined to get her down finally, contorting his face in a fierce grimace as he grasps her arms. She struggles desperately to push him back, protesting breathlessly: 'Oh, no! It's too hot — go away!'

'Why should I go away? You're my wife . . .' Roused

by her resistance, his repressed rage and resentment suddenly mount to frenzy, his eyes flashing blue murder. His expression now is an extraordinary blend of arrogance, lust and fury, with which is mingled something dangerous and demented, reminiscent of a mad dog. ' You'll do as *I* want! ' he snarls, swinging her off her feet, rabid.

Although she writhes and fights and struggles, she has no chance against him, he's so much stronger. In his mad frenzy he flings her down on the bed, holding her there with one arm while the other hand tears off his clothes. She hears the clash of metal when his belt buckle hits the floor, and sees his blue blazing eyes just above her, full of insane dominance and frantic lust.

Down comes his whole hard heavy body then, crushing her flat, the prominent bones digging into her flesh. Now she can struggle no longer, can't even move her head, immobilized by his weight, and his hot mouth glued to hers. Sickened, she's forced to inhale his breath, stinking of whisky, and can only gasp in repulsion. She becomes panic stricken . . . she's suffocating . . . she can't breathe . . . His hot heavy body is hard as rock — a rock overlaid with damp, dank, shaggy fur . . . It's as though a fiery rock from an erupting volcano has fallen on her, and is painfully crushing her to death . . . she can't stand it another second . . . she's dying . . . being horribly murdered . . .

' There, that ought to fix you, my girl,' the man says, with bullying satisfaction. He unglues himself from her, tearing away his sticky, hairy flesh from hers, and stands up by the bed, dripping all over, as though he's just emerged from the sea. Sweat drips from his chin, from his nose and ears, from each drooping hair of the saturated pelt that covers his body, from his dangling fists, and from his limp penis.

For an instant of nightmare panic, she really feels out of her mind, looking up at his well known nudity as at some horrid apparition — a sort of devilish merman, he seems, standing there in triumph, after raping an earthly woman. The rapid flickerings of the light distort everything, and add to the unreality of the scene. She still sees him as an overbearing figure of nightmare as she struggles up, the imprints of his fingers standing out red on her arms, and shakes back her hair, strands of which remain damply plastered to her face and neck. But now his spiteful, gloating expression and crazy grin (exactly like the grin of a mad dog) make her recall what he's just said.

'What do you mean?' She stares at him, blankly uncomprehending at first, gradually growing aghast as what he implies dawns upon her. 'You mean . . . you didn't . . ?'

He nods, with that slightly demented grin, enjoying every moment of her horrified agitation, as she jumps up and flies to the bathroom. 'That's no use!' he calls after her. 'It's too late to do anything now!'

Desperately splashing water, she hears his malicious laugh, followed by a shouted, 'Leave me, would you? I'll teach you!' and then the smack of the door flaps as he goes out. It can't be true, she is thinking . . . this can't really be happening to her . . . she must be having a nightmare . . .

Now that he's gone, she turns back to her room. At this moment, a blinding flash of lightning forks its way down the sky, splitting it apart, its lurid brilliance lighting up every detail: the broken mirror, a few jagged splinters of smashed glass adhering to the frame; the disordered bed and half torn down mosquito net, collapsed in draggled folds on the floor, like the wreckage of an airship disaster; the torn halves of her nightdress, lying among the scattered clothes the man has left where they fell.

As a terrific thunderclap rocks the house, the flickering light dies right down, only recovering partly, so that she's left in near-darkness. Wind gets up with a sudden crash, something outside keeps on frantically banging, the tamarinds make strange rushing noises. She stands bewildered in the midst of all this, rubbing her arms without knowing she's doing so. The glimmer of light is too feeble now to show the red fingerprints, already darkening into bruises; but, by some chance, it does illuminate her dress, and the sandals lying beside it, which she puts on hurriedly and quite mechanically. Lightning is now almost continuous. Vast hollow crashes of wind or thunder fill the darkness, together with the wild rushing noise of the trees.

All of a sudden, in a brief lull, the miniature crash of a glass breaking sounds unexpectedly, startlingly near, to remind her of her husband, drinking in one of the other rooms.

Beginning to tremble a little, she goes to the door, softly pushes the flaps apart, and lets them close soundlessly after her. The man is not in the centre room, but in his bedroom; she hears him shout for his boy from the back window, which faces the servants' quarters. Then, without waiting a second longer, she runs down the stairs, her heelless sandals silent on the bare floors. In any case, the opening and shutting of the front door is inaudible in the uproar of the storm.

Instantly she's sucked out into a black, boiling vortex, a ripping, rushing, thundering bedlam, in which she can't stand, hurled along helplessly by the gale.

A blazing white streak of incandescence splits open the sky, and reveals the solitary palm tree, bent over in a thin, impossible arch, its topmost leaves sweeping the ground like a witch's broom.

## 16

Climbing out of the turmoil of wind and thunder, a slight figure appears on the back porch like a castaway sailor. Sheltered there from the violence of the gale, Mohammed Dirwaza Khan's successor pauses to get his breath, and to adjust his white coat and turban, before going into the house. He doesn't seem quite as impassive as usual as he goes upstairs, carrying in both hands a small brass tray with one tumbler on it. His movements are jerky, and from time to time his eyes roll, so that the white shows all round the black pupil. Moreover, he has omitted to fasten his collar. These manifestations of discomposure are perhaps the result of having been torn away from his private absorbing pursuits and hurriedly dispatched on this unexpected errand; or they may come from a superstitious fear of the storm.

Having set down the glass near his master, who is wearing only a pair of shorts, he starts fumbling with his collar buttons. But the man doesn't even glance at him, ordering him to pick up the shattered remains of the glass he knocked off the table just now.

The youth stoops obediently, his dark hands shaking. One of them, with its paler palm and delicate tapering fingertips, gropes for the broken pieces and puts them on the tray the other hand is still holding. The fragments are scattered all over the floor, and not easily seen in the weak wavering light; it takes him some time, with his imprecise movements, to find them all.

While still engaged in this task, he says, without looking up : ' Missis has gone out.'

In precisely the same tone he might have said, ' Dinner is ready,' or anything else at all. He invariably speaks in the same flat, level voice, so that all his sentences sound alike, whatever their content. Besides, no native servant ever attempts to understand anything about the white people he serves.

On this occasion, it's doubtful whether the meaning of his expressionless words penetrates to his hearer, who merely tells him to send his superior. And, as he has now managed to collect all the broken glass on the tray he at once goes out with it.

The wind brings no coolness; there is no respite from the heat. The night is a black asphyxiating tank, bubbling and steaming. On to the protection of the porch, out of the boiling dark, emerge now, first the long skinny legs, then the rest of the Mohammedan, whose thin grey beard the wind has twisted grotesquely around his neck — his first action is to comb it into place with his fingers.

The youth climbs up after him out of the darkness. And in this order they enter and pass through the house, the leader's lean shanks opening and shutting like giant scissors against the dim light. Without hesitation he goes straight into his master's room and stops in front of him, the youth stopping when he does, just inside the door, where he remains, arms dangling at his sides, a silent, passive appendage of the older man, who has brought him along in case his evidence or corroboration should be required.

' Boy say missis gone out.' His English is less accurate

than his junior's, but he speaks louder and with more assurance, looking the white man full in the face. The youth, on the other hand, looks up at the ceiling, where several small lizards are darting about in confusion, frightened by the thunder, taking short aimless runs which they interrupt suddenly to dash off at a tangent, their tails undulating behind them.

'Boy say he see missis go out.' Getting no answer, Mohammed repeats his sentence in a slightly different form, and with a perceptible note of impatience, which Dog Head is too drunk to notice.

The latter displays no interest or concern, and might not have heard him. He fills the glass to the brim, lifts it, and tips the contents down his throat as if he didn't need to swallow but poured the whisky straight into his stomach. He then puts the glass down empty and speaks a few casual words, ending in English : 'Go after her and bring her to me.' Simultaneously he lifts his hand in a gesture of dismissal, and a fluctuation of the feeble light catches the reddish gleam of the hairs on the back, so that he appears to be wearing a fur-backed glove.

The servant immediately turns round and leaves the room, the youth following, and descends the stairs, his long, thin legs moving as rapidly and silently as a spider's in his scissoring gait.

He says nothing to his subordinate until they are again on the back porch, confronting the turbulent darkness, where the faint glimmerings from their homes are intermittently visible through the tremendous tumult of straining, writhing and streaming branches.

The emotions of both are deeply stirred by the coming of the monsoon — the climax, each year, of their lives. Both resent being distracted from it. For once

Mohammed Dirwaza Khan doesn't mean to obey his master. He hasn't the slightest intention of chasing off after the silly, worthless girl who is his rival — if she's really gone, so much the better; it will spare him the trouble of getting rid of her. This is clearly understood between them; as is the fact that the youth won't go after her either, as he now orders him to do in his place.

The bearded man steps down quickly into the dark stormy turmoil, and is blown along like a scarecrow before the wind, his white garments wildly flapping around him. He doesn't look back to see whether the youth is pretending to obey him, but keeps straight on, rapidly disappearing. The other follows him into the darkness at once, striking out in the direction of his own abode.

If there should be any further disturbance during the night neither of them will hear. The thunder conveniently drowns all lesser noises.

## 17

The loudest thunderclap there has been so far jars the decaying timbers of the house, and one of the lizards drops its tail suddenly, just missing Dog Head's drink. Although it hasn't fallen into the glass, the sight of the tail wriggling madly all round it, before jerking itself off the table and on to the floor, irritates him; he wants to chastise the presumptuous lizard, whose tail he is grinding under his naked heel; but he can't even make out which lizard it belongs to. He feels frustrated, insulted. And now that he's interrupted his heavy drinking, he is in need of an outlet for the violence drink always builds up in him.

He takes the tennis racquet into the next room, where the rats, as disturbed by the storm as the lizards, are immediately in evidence. Constant flashes of lightning increase the distortion caused by the feebly fluttering light, so that the game is extremely chancy. The additional hazard is all on the side of the rats. All the same, it gives the man a fresh thrill, although he has difficulty in following their swift moves, his own movements less co-ordinated than usual owing to the amount of whisky he has consumed, which also seems to affect his judgement. Over-estimating the reach of the racquet, he misses the first rat completely, and has to suffer the humiliation of watching it escape into the rafters. But he makes up for this failure by dispatching the next candidate with one driving blow.

Hardly has he kicked the corpse under the wardrobe

and out of sight than a new rat appears, so enormous that he can scarcely believe his eyes. It disappears in the shadows, and he supposes the distorting properties of the inadequate light must have magnified it to such vast proportions. But no, there it is again; now he sees it quite clearly — a monstrous great brute, with a lion's mane of coarse hair and a tail like a sjambok. Never in all his days has he seen such a colossal rat; it must be the father of all the rats in creation.

He half recalls the ' rat-king ' legend, and that the monster is said to appear to evil-doers when the monsoon breaks; but he at once forgets the story in his excitement, and starts stalking the creature. It won't come into the open, gliding from one piece of furniture to the next, difficult to distinguish from the tremulous shadows. Before long, however, he drives it into a corner, where it crouches under a table, and he knows he's bound to get it when it emerges. ' Come out of there! ' he shouts, furiously banging his fist on the jail-made table, that looks the colour of blood. The rat defies him by refusing to budge, remaining motionless and invisible, except when the occasional gleam of its reddish eyes betrays its presence.

' I'll soon settle you! ' he yells fiercely. The wild excitement by which he's possessed has given him unnatural strength; he swings the table bodily into the air with one hand, while the other twirls the racquet high over his head and brings it down with tremendous force, administering the *coup de grace*. The beast contorts itself with a shrill blood-curdling scream, then rolls over and lies quite still.

He's rather disappointed by this easy victory. The brute ought to have put up a better fight. *Is* it dead?

As it's still in deep shadow and practically hidden he can't be certain, merely assuming it is, as it doesn't move. He steps forward to make sure and to examine the monstrosity.

But before he's had time to look, something moves behind him — turning, he sees a rat of ordinary size calmly crossing the floor, in full view, as if it owned the place. Such unheard of impudence immediately makes him forget the other; he goes in pursuit of this new-comer, hoping to hit it first time, before it takes cover. But again he's misled, either by the flickering light or his own faulty judgement, and the beast eludes him. Now of course it's very much on the alert, and turns out to be almost fiendishly cunning. It persistently keeps out of reach, and when it does emerge from one hiding place to dart to another it's always too quick for him. Exactly as if *it* were playing with *him,* it leads him on to exhaust himself to no purpose, while economizing its own strength, making only such moves as are absolutely essential to avoid his blows.

At first he curses it with all the swear words in his vocabulary; but gradually he falls silent, conserving his breath. He is panting; sweat pours off him in streams; the contest already seems to have lasted for hours. Again and again he's on the point of dealing the fatal blow, but each time something puts him off his stroke — and there's the devilish rat, still waiting for him as large as life.

His excitement wears off by degrees. His blows get wilder and fall wide of the mark. He stumbles once or twice, no longer quite steady on his feet. Though he won't admit it, he's tired, he's had more than enough of the bloody rat, and wishes it would take itself off to hell. Deliberately giving it a chance, he pauses to mop his face. But instead of flying up the wall to the security of the rafters the diabolical creature continues to lead him on, darting here, there, and everywhere, always evading him. Not once has he even managed to touch the brute.

All at once it vanishes under the table, swallowed up by the shadows. But its eyes give it away, glinting malevolently as they reflect the light's fluctuations. He waits for it to move, breathing in hoarse gasps, but with a triumphant face. At last the rat's made the same mistake as its predecessor, and will meet the same end as soon as it comes out. He does nothing to hasten the fate of this one, glad of the respite in which to collect what remains of his strength for the final effort.

The moment the beast starts to slide out of the corner he lunges at it with all his force, savagely shouting, ' Got you! '

But he never knows whether he really has killed, or even hit it, for at the same time he staggers wildly, losing his balance, his arms flailing. Unable to save himself he falls headlong, sprawling full length on the floor, face downwards, on top of the object that's tripped him up. He must be slightly stunned, in his drunken state, by the heaviness of the fall, for he doesn't get up immediately, doesn't know what he's fallen over.

An inexplicable, indescribable movement rouses him : hairs coarse as wire are scratching his chest, neck and chin. With sudden horror, he realizes that he must have tripped over and be lying on top of the monster rat, which he'd completely forgotten until this moment. And the beast's moving . . . it's come to life . . . Its cold sharp claws scrabble at his chest, becoming entangled in its furlike growth, as he struggles desperately to get hold of it — somehow, he's unable to throw it off; there's no power in his hands, which can't get a grip on its body . . .

Precisely as in a nightmare, he feels its teeth sinking into his throat. He can't see it properly, though its heavy limp inert shape dangles in front of him, hanging on by its teeth and claws . . . while he beats at it ineffectually, his blue eyes frantically glaring about the room — he shouts for help, but nobody answers . . .

He must get up in order to get a firmer grip. But his strength is going, and though he makes a terrific effort he only succeeds in dragging himself to his knees. Blood is streaming over his chest, mingling with the river of sweat.

After a final flicker, the light goes out. Seeing only some huge black object looming above him, he clutches it to pull himself up. The wardrobe starts to wobble and sway before he gets to his feet; his fingers, sticky with blood, adhere to the tacky surface, pulling it down on him. Like a giant coffin, it falls with a crash, imprisoning him in stifling darkness beneath — in the dustbin to which he consigns his victims.

As if the bottom has fallen out of the sky, rain comes down with a thunderous smash. Pounding on the roof, the vast mass of water adds its continuous battering boom to the ponderous roar of great thunder-wheels rolling loose in the blackness outside.

All lesser noises are hopelessly lost in this ceaseless bludgeoning of tumultuous noise.

## 18

It is very early, not yet day. In the east the leaden clouds have parted, exposing a segment of slowly brightening sky. Soon the clouds will come together again in combat, crashing and thundering against one-another, flooding the world with rain as with their life blood. But first there is this moment of peace, a fugitive breath of coolness, a pause which belongs to neither night nor day.

The purple-blue of the sky slowly lightens to pure piercing turquoise, a shade only seen at this hour, and for a few seconds only, before the sunrise. Light grows imperceptibly, infiltrating the shades of night.

The servants are still asleep in their own quarters after the excitement of the monsoon's arrival. The house stands silent, as if deserted; the open shutters reveal only black holes of rooms. Last night's bath has emphasized its latent dilapidation; the neglected exterior is more noticeable, the cracks in the walls, and the splintering woodwork. What is not seen is the more serious secret damage, where termites have undermined and eroded, so that, unaccountably, objects come crashing down.

The solitary palm tree in front looks battered, be-draggled and shabby, among pools of rain water left in the hollows of the uneven ground. The swamp has changed colour overnight like a conjuring trick, covered in bright blue flowers. Almost visibly, new green shoots are everywhere piercing the newly sodden earth, from which mist slowly steams up and hangs in long trails just above the ground. A soundless procession of yellow-robed begging priests passes, ankle deep in the white vapour, ghostly and transient as a dream.

Frcm the sheltered recesses of the forest trees the great snake moves slowly towards the light and negligently loops its pale length, swaying gently from side to side. Those of the small parrots which have survived the storm's bombardment are waking with drowsy wing-stretchings, so many handfuls of brilliant feathers that seem barely held together by the frail thread of life.

Who-are-you? Who-are-you? Who-are-you? The brain-fever bird's harsh cry is always the first definite sound to be heard, although the birds themselves remain mysteriously invisible among the sparse foliage and involved tracery of the tamarind branches. All day long their interminable unanswered question will continue, an irritating inescapable background noise, mingling with every second, with all situations, weaving its way into the whole human fabric of talk, thought and action, until the sudden curtain of darkness falls.

Who-are-you? Who-are-you? Who-are-you? The same loud insistent cry is transmitted from bird to bird in a whole succession of identical but more remote cries, coming, not only from the vicinity of the house, but from much further afield : from the other side of the road, from all over the confused tract of country beyond, even from the distant jungle where thousands of the same species must congregate. Some of these ceaseless cries are louder than others, or more prolonged : but all alike share the common exasperating suggestion of a mechanical noise nobody can stop; they don't express hunger, or love, or fear, or anything else, but seem uttered with the sole object of maddening whoever hears them.

The tops of the tamarinds suddenly burn, fiery; the sun is up, gilding the topmost point of the roof. Instantly the air fills with the shrill, continuous din of innumerable insects of every kind, which at once seems always to have been going on.

Countless birds, too, explode into screaming, whistling, whooping or chattering cries, impossible to disentangle. Darting to and fro, the small parrots trace complex emerald diagrams on the air, their thin screeching lost in the general commotion which is called silence.

From this confusion of noise, only the cries of the brain-fever birds emerge distinctly, nerve-racking and unmistakably clear, violently assaulting the ears with their loud, flat repetitions, like mechanical instruments of torture.

They implant an obscure irritant in the brain, eternally calling out the monotonous question nobody will ever answer, from all points of the compass, from far and near . . . which others of their kind infuriatingly echo . . . and others still . . . driving the crazed hearer into delirium . . . until the ultimate nightmare climax — when suddenly everything stops . . .

## 19

Suède Boots drops in for tea as usual, cheerful, smiling, matter of fact. At once the girl feels happier and more relaxed. She's become much more tranquil under his influence.

But she's still nervous about her husband, who has now recovered, and spends most of the time working in his office. He hasn't said a word to her about the daily visits, which strikes her as ominous, sinister. She can't believe Suède Boots is right in saying that, by keeping silent, he shows he has no objection.

Not that there's anything for him to object to. Their relationship is perfectly innocent. Anybody might listen to their conversation, even when it's personal. Their intimacy has not progressed beyond an almost childish enjoyment of being together, exchanging smiles, talking nonsense, or, alternatively, discussing life with great seriousness.

'Before I met you I used to feel as if I was in a nightmare,' she tells him, 'and that I'd never escape.' But she no longer remembers this feeling with any distinctness, and might be describing the sensations of a girl in a book.

Sometimes she has an uneasy sense of the precariousness of the present situation, and is afraid her new happiness may vanish suddenly. But she refuses to admit this or to think about it, though it shows itself in her superstitious desire to keep everything between them exactly the same as it always has been — she can't bear any change to creep in.

The young man is really fond of her and concerned for her welfare. He has made up his mind that her unsuitable marriage must end; then she'll be able to go to the university as she's always wanted. Whether their relationship is supposed to become closer eventually is not very clear in his mind. But he's taken the step of writing to his family about her, so that she can stay with them, as she's got nobody to take care of her over there.

She is touched when she hears this — gratitude overwhelms her. She's never known so much kindness existed in life. Carried away by his enthusiasm she eagerly discusses her future with him. They make up all sorts of different plans, each leading to a fresh favourable outcome. For the possibilites seem endless, each more glowing than the last. So that she gets quite excited about them; excitement perhaps goes to her head a little.

But as soon as her excitement dies down, the whole project begins to seem unreal. She can't believe it will ever come off. Things don't happen like that in her case — they always go wrong.

' It's just a fairy tale you've made up about me — it can't possibly come true.' Thus she demolishes all the plans they have been constructing together. It's no good inventing a happy future for her, since she's always been unlucky, and always will be.

Silence falls after this. The young man is disappointed; but he won't give up, and is now thinking how he can persuade her to take a more optimistic view. She has told him she'd like to live through their original meeting all over again, so he asks if she remembers their conversation then. 'We said that if I hadn't killed the snake on that particular day, and you hadn't happened to see me, everything would have been quite different.' He sees her looking at him with interest, and is encouraged to go on. 'I wouldn't be here with you now. This wouldn't be real — something else would. You'd have been another you, instead of the one you are now. You can't be tied down to a predestined fate when you change according to your situation, and your fate must change too. Everything depends on circumstances — on which " you " you happen to be at a given time . . . '

Interrupting exactly as if it wanted to join in, a brain-fever bird just outside starts shouting, Who-are-you? so loudly that no human voice can compete with it. He can only wait for it to stop. They smile at each other, sitting helplessly, while the monotonous, everlasting question is taken up by all the brain-fever birds for miles around. The girl can't even think about what he's been saying — though it sounded reasonable, she has a vague idea there's a flaw in the argument somewhere. But she can't detect it with this row going on — she's never heard the birds make such a din.

Loud, flat and persistent, the repetitious cries come from all distances and directions, filling the room, the house, the whole afternoon with their exasperating sound, which expresses no normal bird-feeling, but seems only meant to drive people mad. Like mad machines nobody can stop, the birds go on and on. Their deafening chorus hammers upon her nerves until she's half dazed.

This no doubt explains why she's slower than her companion to hear the new mechanical noise he heard several seconds ago — she becomes aware of it first when she sees that the smile's disappeared from his face. Now she strains her ears to follow the low continuous hum or buzz through the birds' commotion, and has barely identified it as the noise of a car when it stops abruptly.

Everything else seems to stop with it. The bird-calls abruptly break off. In the ensuing silence, footsteps are heard approaching, loud, heavy, regular as machinery. The door flaps fly open to admit Mr Dog Head, who doesn't speak but stands staring at the pair, a curious blend of indignation, contempt and triumph on his arrogant features. He's delighted to have caught his wife in the act — of what, he doesn't trouble to think, but tells himself that now he really has something to blame her for. For the moment, however, he concentrates his offensive gaze on the visitor, who gets up in confusion and holds out his hand.

Dog Head looks down his supercilious nose at him in amazed contempt, as much as to say, ' Good God ! Surely this scum of the earth doesn't expect me to touch him '— he'd never dream of contaminating his lordly self in this way ! But aloud he says nothing, merely continuing to glare at the hand, until its owner withdraws it, muttering something incomprehensible in his indignation at the silent insolence of the man's behaviour — who the hell does he think he is, standing there as if he expected people to fall down and worship him ?

Restraining his anger, the guest decides that the most dignified course is to shame him by his own politeness, and says : ' I'm glad we've met finally; I've always missed you before. Our office hours must be different.'

Not a word comes in response to this. A lengthy pause follows, and then he goes on, although the other has shown not the slightest interest, ' We have to start early, but then we get off early too,' embarking on a rather detailed account of his work schedule, which would be more appropriate if he'd been questioned about it. Not a single inquiry is made, and no comment either. The man he's talking to simply goes on staring at him with the same contemptuous arrogance; until his personal servant brings in a fresh pot of tea, and he sits down and pours himself a cup, taking no more notice of Suède Boots than if he were a fly buzzing round the ceiling. Apparently he doesn't hear a word he is saying, not even glancing at him now, his over-bearing countenance fixed in stony disdainful in-difference, as if he'd been petrified with this expression.

Catching sight of his face, the young fellow suddenly interrupts himself, his own face turning scarlet. He looks like a furious little boy, but chokes back the angry words on his lips and turns to the girl instead, saying, ' Well, I'll be off now.' He smiles at her with a cheerful-ness he is far from feeling, then hurries out, the smile changing to a grimace as soon as he turns his back.

Humiliated, enraged and embarrassed, he leaves the house as fast as he can. Something makes him glance back at it over his shoulder while crossing the compound, and he sees a tall, gaunt bearded figure posted outside the door like a sentry, watching him off the premises. The same grimace, openly furious now, crosses his face. Soon he is out of sight.

The squeak of the fan gets louder and louder in the room where husband and wife have been left alone. The man has turned all his anger against her now. But she's only thinking about the sudden end of her happi-ness, which she has always feared — she seems to have known all along that things would end like this. Despair has fallen upon her. She hardly cares what happens. Of course there's bound to be an appalling row. She waits almost indifferently for it to begin. She's disgusted by her husband's rudeness to her friend and repelled by him when she catches a glimpse accidentally of his staring blue eyes, like a pair of marbles in his tanned face. The red ring his hat has left round his forehead might be a royal symbol, judging by his high and mighty expression. She can't stand this assumption of superiority after the way he's been behaving, and instinctively picks up a book and pretends to read, so that she needn't see him.

Naturally, this enrages him even more. ' What were you doing alone with that young whippersnapper? ' he asks in a bullying tone.

' Now it's coming,' she thinks helplessly. But she says nothing. What's the use of talking to him?

' Answer me! ' He jumps up and stands over her, his fist coming down in a nerve-shattering thump on the table, making the cups jump and rattle and slop the dregs of cold tea into their saucers.

The agonizing squeak of the fan seems to be trying in vain to drown the noise of his heavy breathing. She knows the superior look she can't stand must be on his face, so she doesn't look up or see how strangely his eyes are glittering. ' We were having tea.' She can hardly bring herself to answer him, and speaks the words with difficulty.

But to the hearer her low voice sounds indifferent. It certainly isn't apologetic — this and the way she refuses to look at him drives him nearly frantic. ' What sort of a bloody fool do you take me for? ' he explodes. ' Do you imagine I don't know you've been seeing him every day?'

Is she really expected to answer this? It seems too idiotic. Although she still hasn't raised her head she's aware all the time of him looming over her menacingly, and feels somewhat apprehensive. She wouldn't mind if he'd kill her outright, but is afraid he may beat her up. At the same time, he seems quite insignificant — her friendship with Suède Boots is responsible for the new and more critical attitude she adopts towards him. He seems like some base object, repulsive and disgusting, with his incredible arrogance — where in the world did he get this grotesquely high opinion of himself? Let him do the quarrelling — she's not going to argue. Overwhelmed by the utter futility of saying anything to him, since he neither listens nor understands, she simply remains silent.

The man thinks she's provoking him intentionally — trying to drive him out of his mind — by not apologizing or even speaking. The glint in his eyes can't be described as normal, as he shouts at her: 'He's not to come into the house again — ever! Do you hear?' She still doesn't open her mouth even now, and he seizes her by the shoulders and shakes her violently to and fro, as if to shake it open, but only succeeds in shaking the book out of her hand. 'I won't have him walking past the compound either — if he does, I'll set the chuprassi on him!' Hardly knowing what he's saying he adds a few more abusive, threatening phrases at random, while continuing to shake her furiously.

But after a moment he begins to feel baffled, deflated. He can't go on shaking her for ever, and he has no idea what else to do. He can't discover any way of forcing his will upon her. It's absolutely maddening to be so frustrated : but there seems to be nothing he can do about it. The next thing is that he has to let her go.

Still she hasn't uttered one word of apology, contrition, or anything else. All that's happened is that her hair has been shaken loose and falls forward untidily, the fine, freshly-washed hair separating into two masses, one on each side of her face, which it hides completely, showing only the back of her neck.

Gazing down at the pale nape of her neck, extended before him like that of a victim, he feels the mounting pressure of violence inside him, a rabid frenzy of rage which frightens him suddenly — all at once he's afraid of what it might make him do. Swinging round abruptly he strides away from her and out of the room.

It is evening, after dinner. The girl is sitting reading, alone under the squeaky fan. Her husband hasn't spoken to her all day. The few remarks he made at the dinner table were for the benefit of the servants, before whom a façade of normal conduct must be maintained. She doesn't know where he is now, or what he is doing. He may be somewhere in the house. Or he may have gone to the club. She hasn't heard the car drive away, but this doesn't necessarily mean he's still here, as he sometimes walks this short distance.

He is not in the habit of telling her when he goes out. He seems to keep her in ignorance of his movements deliberately, hoping to take her by surprise, as he's done occasionally when she's been relaxing under the impression that she was alone in the house. It's as though he perpetually suspects her of doing wrong, and is eagerly waiting to catch her in the act again. This is why her attitude remains tense. She keeps her eyes unwaveringly on her book, although the light is really too faint for reading. Presently she puts the book down on a table and rubs her eyes, afterwards sitting quite still, her wide open eyes looking towards the door.

The noise of the frogs fills the night, as the brain-fever birds' cries fill the day. The two sounds are interchangeable in her head, composing one continuous, exasperating background sound, without end or beginning, that finds its way into every single second of the day and night. Not for one of all those seconds has she ever felt at home in this house. She has no clear impression of the darkened country outside; it is to her just a feeling of alien, burning brilliance, heat and confusion, and of mysterious nocturnal cries that burst unaccountably out of solid blackness.

Her gaze does not leave the door, and now, under the two flaps, in the lighted passage beyond, she sees a pair of slim brown ankles approaching, and the border of the red skirt belonging to the young woman who looks after her clothes, prepares her bath, and so on, who, unlike the Mahommedans, is a native of the country. Her appearance so late in the evening is puzzling, since she is off duty and ought to be at home.

There is a certain elegance about the red skirt, shot with gold, above which is worn an exceedingly abbreviated white jacket, a wide expanse of smooth brown flesh exposed between the two garments. The wearer's movements are supple, graceful and self-possessed. Although her face has not got the blank look worn by most of the other servants, it is no more accessible; its expression, lively but unconcerned, seems to impose a sheet of glass between her and her mistress, who is several years younger. She looks at her amicably but remotely, keeping herself apart, unapproachable. Or perhaps it is the girl who has never made any attempt to approach her. At all events, there is no contact between them.

' The other master has come.' This announcement is made in a soft voice that might sound cautious, were it not for the calm, matter of fact way the speaker is adjusting the comb which controls her long coil of oiled hair, black and shiny as patent leather.

The words are so totally unexpected that the girl looks at her with a startled face, uncomprehending. A familiar voice then calls to her softly from outside the room : ' Come out here for a second — I must speak to you ! '

Immediately she jumps up and runs to the window giving access to the verandah, passing the messenger without seeing her, not giving her another thought. The latter quietly closes the shutters after she's gone out, then leaves the room through the door she's just entered, moving with her soft, loose gait, and swaying her hips, the soles of her light slippers (worn with the little toe outside the embroidered upper part) hitting the floor with a muffled slap that is hard to hear above the noise the frogs make.

The girl's progress along the dark verandah can be followed by the very similar slight slap of her sandals on the wooden floor. The soft-soled mosquito boots advancing to meet her make no noise at all, even when the frog chorus is silenced momentarily by one exceptionally deep croaking boom, after which it at once starts again.

It's pitch dark out here, without a breath of air. There is no moon. The faint ghostly sheen of starlight over the swamp doesn't reach to the compound. Only a thin pencilling of parallel light lines marks the position of shuttered windows. The roofed verandah is like a black tunnel of airless heat, where the paleness of clothes, faces and limbs can only be guessed at, not even discernible as lighter blurs on the black.

'What are you doing here? You must go at once,' the girl whispers, terrified Dog Head will spring out at them like a jack in the box.

'It's all right — I gave that girl of yours a present to tell me when the coast was clear.'

This reference to the forgotten messenger fills the hearer with admiration for the practical attitude it indicates, far better at coping with life than her own. But then fear seizes her again, she glances round nervously, murmuring : 'But I'm not sure that he's out of the house . . . he may be around somewhere . . .'

'You simply must leave him.' Suède Boots' muted voice might be addressed to an accomplice; or he might be anxious to avoid waking a sleeper nearby. 'The fellow's quite mad. He ought to be locked up. You're not safe with him. Promise you'll come to my place tomorrow.'

But it is *his* safety that's uppermost in her mind, or else she doesn't want to commit herself, for instead of answering she says urgently : 'You mustn't walk along the path any more — or he'll do something awful . . .'

'Oh, so he's threatened me, has he?' Indignation raises the young man's voice half a tone. But her urgent, 'Hush!' quietens him, and she can only just hear when he starts talking fast, as if against time : 'Don't forget, I'll be waiting for you — you've got to come. You can't possibly stay on here. I tell you what —

to remind you, I'll fix a scarf or something on the snake's tree. You're bound to see it there whenever you look out. That ought to stop you sliding back into that nightmare of yours. Don't worry. Lots of people want to help you. Only you must make the first move yourself. You must leave here — soon! ' The last words are spoken more slowly and emphatically, like a teacher impressing an important lesson upon an inattentive pupil.

Their hands have met in the darkness. His touch is so comforting and reassuring to her that it absorbs the attention she ought to be giving to what he says. Now, however, her hand is relinquished. The blur of his white shirt, which she's just able to make out while he's standing in front of her, rapidly recedes, melting into the darkness without a trace.

She is left alone with the frogs, whose chorus is mounting to a crescendo. It's quite impossible for her to see which way Suède Boots has gone, even though she leans far over the rail under the trailing orchids to peer into the hot black night.

Now it becomes almost too hot to live as the monsoon approaches. Each afternoon great menacing masses of cloud gather and roof over the world, which swelters beneath, in burning suspense and tension.

The girl is still not acclimatized, and can't stand this terrific heat, which keeps her awake at night, so that she's always tired. If only she could go to some cool place! But, in spite of her longing to get away, she does nothing about it, feeling vaguely that the time hasn't come yet.

Suède Boots has hung a blue scarf on the tree to remind her that kind people exist who will help and accept her. She remembers him saying, ' Don't worry — all my family will love you.' She has such a craving for love that she often dreams of staying with them, and even thinks she will really go sometime — at some dim future date. But, as the torrid days slowly pass, the idea grows more and more dreamlike, and the people seem less and less real. Every day she believes in them a little less, since he can't come any more to talk to her and convince her of their reality.

Her husband doesn't talk to her either. For days at a time she speaks to no one except the servants. She is always lonely, and always seems to be waiting, but isn't sure whether she's waiting for the monsoon, or to escape, or just for another day. All the days are the same to her now, and they are all empty of everything but discomfort.

The heat is an abominable infliction that takes away all her vitality.

Tonight she's entirely alone in the house. Dog Head is out in the car. The servants have gone, and won't come back till the morning. It is late, but the night seems to get hotter, even hotter than the day. The air is so oppressive that she can hardly move. At last she drags herself up to her room, takes her clothes off, and, stunned into apathy, sits on the bed under the fan, doing nothing. The dim light flickers the whole time. Her head aches, her eyes burn, she can't make the effort of reading a book. Lightning is flickering too on the backs of her silver brushes, lying there like relics of a lost life. She's dead tired, but knows she won't be able to sleep — in any case, it's far too hot to lie down. She has the sensation of dropping into a great steamy tank of asphyxiating heat.

Suddenly she comes to with a violent start, just as her husband appears in the room without warning. His hostile overbearing face comes towards her, he is flourishing a sheet of paper, demanding, ' What's the meaning of this? ' as he waves it in front of her.

She recognizes the letter that came from the university some time ago — how on earth can he have discovered it in its secret hiding place? she wonders, too dazed and disconcerted to answer. ' So you're planning to rat on me,' she hears next. The word rat makes her shudder, uttered in that bullying voice. But, still half stupefied, she only shrinks away from him without speaking.

It's not the letter he's so angry about really. But she has no conception of the outrage she's committed by making a fool of him — as he thinks — by her friendship with Suède Boots, and not even apologizing for it. It

never occurs to her, in her innocence, that she owes
him an apology. She's quite unaware of how insulted he
feels; and her oblivious attitude infuriates him still
more.

'Why don't you answer?' he shouts, grasping her
arms so violently that, unprepared, she slides off the
edge of the bed, falling against him. He has been
drinking as usual. She smells the whisky on his breath
and twists her head away, trying to push him back.
But he won't release her, roused by the contact with
her nakedness. She feels lust rising in him, which is
mainly the lust to conquer her, and starts struggling.
His blue, blazing, lustful eyes are quite close to hers;
now, for the first time, she sees in them something
dangerous and demented, reminding her of a mad dog,
and strains away from him with all her strength. But of
course she has no chance against him. He is far too
strong. Overpowering her easily, he throws her on to the
bed. Then down comes his big, sweating body on top
of her, crushing her flat. Thunder crashes at the same
moment, and, in her confused state, it's as if the thunder
has hurled itself on her, rolling its immensity over her
and holding her down, while lightning transfixes her with
a piercing pain. She can't breathe — the man's mouth,
fixed on hers, stops her breathing. She's suffocating . . .
dying . . . she's being murdered . . .

Just when she can't endure it another second, Dog
Head removes his weight from her and stands up by
the bed. Dimmed by the lightning, the flickering light
gives him a frightening, unreal, unfamiliar aspect that's
hardly human. He stands over her with that rabid
expression, showing his teeth in a mad dog's grin. In
the midst of the atrocious heat she shivers with sudden

chill, seeing him, not as her husband at all, but as some nightmare horror — a dog-headed man. Suddenly she's panic-stricken — she must escape immediately, and at all costs . . .

His appetite and his rage sated for the moment, the husband goes off for a drink, leaving her alone. She gets her clothes on somehow and rushes out, across the centre room, down the stairs, the slight sound of her steps drowned by the storm. In her panic, she has only one thought : to get out of the house, and away from the man who's half nightmare. Thunder goes on all the time. The lightning keeps stabbing at the windows, as if trying to reach her. A blinding flash stops her as she gets to the door, ripping the sky apart, followed by a tremendous thunderclap, shaking the house.

But now she abruptly returns to normal. Panic leaves her as soon as she opens the door and sees the way open before her. No longer under such desperate pressure of need to be gone, she pauses in the porch, noticing, with amazement, that what Suède Boots said is quite true — all she has to do is to walk out of the place, exactly as he always told her. How simple it seems. The thing she's thought almost impossible, when it comes to the point, is really perfectly easy.

But she still doesn't move, though nothing to do with the storm keeps her standing there : perhaps it's her belief in her own unchangeable bad luck; or perhaps a constitutional fear of any decisive step. Holding on to the door so that it shan't slam shut in the wind, she turns her head and looks towards the stairs behind her, as though she might decide to go back to her room after all.

Then she turns again, and another flash zigzags down

the sky, illuminating the compound with white incandescence, showing the palm tree bent over in a thin impossible arc, its topmost leaves sweeping the ground. It looks like a hallucination. Everything out there has the same fantastic, improbable aspect, as if it were part of a fever-dream. The well-known landmarks are hardly recognizable.

Her eyes, dazzled by the livid glare of the lightning, suddenly start to search the weird scene with a new, acute urgency. On the spur of the moment, she's made up her mind that chance shall decide her fate. She will go if she succeeds in seeing the scarf before the lurid light expires. Otherwise she'll stay.

In his room, Dog Head drinks steadily for some time. A lizard drops its tail near his glass, and he jumps up indignantly to pursue it. It has disappeared. But now that he's interrupted his drinking he feels in need of an outlet for the violence drink always builds up in him.

He takes his racquet into the next room, where the combination of lightning and the weak electricity greatly increases the difficulties of the rat game. Moreover, he himself is not completely steady on his feet, and is apt to misjudge distances. He lashes out wildly at each rat that shows itself, missing more often than not.

The stifling heat seems to be inside him, rather than out. Everything is dark in his mind, which is filled with furious resentment against his wife. He's really hitting out at her, not the rats, as he slashes the racquet at them with all his strength. He shouts to her to come and watch him playing, but of course she doesn't reply. He would go and drag her out of her room, if he were not fully occupied here. Playing in this extravagant, imprecise way, he soon exhausts himself; sweat is running off him like water.

Though he won't admit it, he's really had more than enough of the game, when an unusually large rat comes on the scene, and eludes him persistently, almost driving him crazy. At last he corners it, and, with a yell of triumph, brings the racquet down in a vicious drive. But once again he miscalculates. Lunging forward, he staggers, losing his balance, starting to fall, and, to save himself, clutches at some piece of furniture, which tilts over on top of him, bearing him to the ground with it.

It is not the ponderous, blood-red wardrobe made in the jail, but a light affair constructed of laths. Nevertheless, he cries out in a loud and agonized voice for someone to help him. No one answers. Nobody comes. The servants don't hear, or don't want to hear.

His wife must have heard — surely she's bound to come to the rescue. His rage dissolves in self-pity, he whimpers drunkenly to himself, lying under the cupboard, because she doesn't appear either. For a time, he can think of nothing but his own pathetic position. Nobody cares that he's crushed under an oppressive weight, in darkness and misery.

As soon as he makes the effort, of course, he dislodges the cupboard quite easily. Immediately then his anger revives, flaring up again, as he gets to his feet, bruised and shaken, and makes for the girl's room. It's absolutely intolerable that she should have left him lying there helpless all that time without lifting a finger, and he means to take some violent revenge. He will do something terrible to her — perhaps kill her.

All at once, just as he gets to the door, his strength

and his furious anger desert him together; he seems to fall in on himself, to disintegrate almost, and slowly subsides to the floor, overcome by profound exhaustion.

The night is almost over, though he has lost all sense of time. The thunder recedes into the distance and slowly dies out. He listens intently in the new stillness, but there's no sound or sign of life on the other side of the door.

This is the point when the clouds start to break up, leaving a gap in the east, where soon the sun will appear. The electricity expired in the house long ago. But now the black window squares are growing brighter. A vague huddled shape, indicated by the pallor of his shorts and his naked flesh, the man half lies on the floor, his head and shoulders propped against the wall, between the wardrobe and the door of his wife's room. He is motionless, except when his chin intermittently drops on his chest as he falls into a brief doze, or wakes with a sudden start.

He does not move from this spot, and, whenever he remembers to do so, goes on listening. The door flaps constitute no sort of a barrier against noise; yet all this time there has been no sound on the other side loud enough to reach him. The occupant of the room must be keeping quiet deliberately; or else sleeping soundly. It is also possible that she is not there at all and that the room is empty.

At length Dog Head leaves his place at the door without investigating the room beyond. Too tired to care about the girl now, he falls on his own bed, and is asleep instantly, with his mouth slightly open.

The light intensifies outside the windows, which are already luminous. Suddenly the sun leaps into the sky, gilding the tops of the tamarinds and the highest point of the roof. At once the brain-fever birds fill the air with their monotonous cries, as if they had never stopped mechanically calling out the eternal question no one will ever answer.

In their quarters, the servants are still sleeping off the excitements of the night. The dilapidated house stands silent, as if deserted, in the almost cool air of daybreak; as though it were already an abandoned ruin, empty, and fallen into decay. The rooms appear as so many black holes through the unshuttered, wide open windows.

## DAVID CALLARD

The Case of Anna Kavan:
*A Biography*

'It is a challenging task to unlock the secret cabinet of Anna Kavan,' said Brian Aldiss. In *The Case of Anna Kavan* biographer David Callard has made a fine, sensitive and illuminating attempt to unlock that cabinet, to unravel the life of the self-proclaimed 'thrilling enigma for posterity'.

Kavan destroyed most of her personal correspondence and all of her diaries, save those covering an eighteen-month period – and even these she doctored and falsified – so to separate fact from fantasy is a near-impossible task. But Callard has done just that, shining a light into the dark, obsessive world of Kavan's imagination and detailing her extraordinary life and equally extraordinary work, her forty-year heroin addiction, her switches of identity, her deep depressions and her suicide attempts.

He reveals a woman at odds with the world around her and with life's 'hateful and tiresome dream'. Yet she channelled these feelings into a body of work that defies categorization and stands as one of the most singular in twentieth-century British literature. The surreal, apocalyptic, hallucinatory style of her writing often borders on poetry, and the realm of numbness and paranoia she depicts can only come from her own experience.

'This determination to be, as she put it, "the world's best-kept secret" presents the biographer with a difficult task, which Callard has accomplished remarkably well.'
– Francis King, *Spectator*

'David Callard's well-written biography has all the facts.'
– *The Times*

'Callard provides perceptive analyses of Kavan's many novels and short stories.'
– *Times Literary Supplement*

'Callard, who has left no stone unturned, shows himself to be both a brilliant researcher and a biographer of the highest order.'
– *The Tablet*

'Callard is an excellent biographer and clever detective.'
– *UCL Book Review*

0 7206 0867 8
cased
illustrated
£16.95

## ANNA KAVAN
### Asylum Piece

'If only one knew of what and by whom one were accused, when, where and by what laws one were to be judged, it would be possible to prepare one's defence systematically and set about things in a sensible fashion.'

First published sixty years ago, *Asylum Piece* today ranks as one of the most extraordinary and terrifying evocations of human madness ever written.

'Anyone who has ever had an experience of mental illness, or even just a whisper that there is something "other" and evil out there, will find in these stories a kind of reassurance that someone else has been there, too, and has bravely suffered and made something beautiful, clever – and often darkly funny – out of anguish.'
– Virginia Ironside, *Daily Mail*

'A writer of unusual imaginative power'
– Edwin Muir

'An artist of great distinction'
– L.P. Hartley

This collection of stories, mostly interlinked and largely autobiographical, chart the descent of the narrator from the onset of neurosis to final incarceration in a Swiss clinic. The sense of paranoia, of persecution by a foe or force that is never given a name, evokes *The Trial* by Kafka, a writer with whom Kavan is often compared, although her deeply personal, restrained and almost foreign-accented style has no true model. The same characters who recur throughout – the protagonist's unhelpful 'adviser', the friend/lover who abandons her at the clinic and an assortment of deluded companions – are sketched without a trace of the rage, self-pity or sentiment that have marked more recent accounts of mental instability.

0 7206 1123 7
paperback
£9.95

# ANNA KAVAN

## The Parson

*The Parson* was not published in Anna Kavan's lifetime but was found after her death in manuscript form. Thought to have been written between the mid-1950s and early 1960s, it presages, through its undertones and imagery, some of Kavan's later and most enduring fiction, particularly her novel *Ice*. It was published finally, to wide acclaim, by Peter Owen in 1995.

The Parson of the title is not a cleric but an upright young army officer so nicknamed for his apparent prudishness. On leave in his native homeland, he meets Rejane, a rich and beguiling beauty, the woman of his dreams. The days that the Parson spends with Rejane, riding in and exploring the wild moorland, have their own enchantment, but Rejane grows restless in this desolate landscape. Although doubtless in love with the Parson, she discourages any intimacy, until she persuades him to take her to a sinister castle situated on a treacherous headland . . .

*The Parson* is less a tale of unrequited love than an exploration of divided selves, momentarily locked in an unequal embrace. Passion is revealed as a play of the senses as well as a destructive force. Valid comparisons have been made between Kavan and Poe, Kafka and Thomas Hardy, but the presence of her trademark themes, cleverly juxtaposed and set in her risk-taking prose, mark *The Parson* as one-hundred-per-cent Kavan.

0 7206 1140 7
paperback
£8.95

If you have enjoyed this book you may like to try some of the other Peter Owen paperback reprints listed below. The **Peter Owen Modern Classics** series was launched in 1998 to bring some of our internationally acclaimed authors and their works, first published by Peter Owen in hardback, to a modern readership.

## Peter Owen Modern Classics

| | | | |
|---|---|---|---|
| **Guillaume Apollinaire** | *Les Onze Mille Verges* | 0 7206 1100 8 | £9.95 |
| **Paul Bowles** | *Midnight Mass* | 0 7206 1083 4 | £9.95 |
| **Paul Bowles** | *Points in Time* | 0 7206 1137 7 | £8.50 |
| **Paul Bowles** | *Their Heads Are Green* | 0 7206 1077 X | £9.95 |
| **Paul Bowles** | *Up Above the World* | 0 7206 1087 7 | £9.95 |
| **Blaise Cendrars** | *To the End of the World* | 0 7206 1097 4 | £9.95 |
| **Jean Cocteau** | *Le Livre Blanc* | 0 7206 1081 8 | £8.50 |
| **Colette** | *Duo and Le Toutounier* | 0 7206 1069 9 | £9.95 |
| **Lawrence Durrell** | *Pope Joan* | 0 7026 1065 6 | £9.95 |
| **Shusaku Endo** | *Wonderful Fool* | 0 7206 1080 X | £9.95 |
| **Hermann Hesse** | *Demian* | 0 7206 1130 X | £9.95 |
| **Hermann Hesse** | *Journey to the East* | 0 7206 1131 8 | £8.50 |
| **Hermann Hesse** | *Narcissus and Goldmund* | 0 7206 1102 4 | £12.50 |
| **Anna Kavan** | *Asylum Piece* | 0 7206 1123 7 | £9.95 |
| **Anna Kavan** | *The Parson* | 0 7206 1140 7 | £8.95 |
| **Anna Kavan** | *Sleep Has His House* | 0 7206 1129 6 | £9.95 |
| **Anna Kavan** | *Who Are You?* | 0 7206 1150 4 | £8.95 |
| **Yukio Mishima** | *Confessions of a Mask* | 0 7206 1031 1 | £11.95 |
| **Anaïs Nin** | *Collages* | 0 7206 1145 8 | £9.95 |
| **Anaïs Nin** | *The Four-Chambered Heart* | 0 7206 1155 5 | £9.95 |
| **Boris Pasternak** | *The Last Summer* | 0 7206 1099 0 | £8.50 |
| **Cesare Pavese** | *The Devil in the Hills* | 0 7206 1118 0 | £9.95 |
| **Cesare Pavese** | *The Moon and the Bonfire* | 0 7206 1119 9 | £9.95 |
| **Mervyn Peake** | *A Book of Nonsense* | 0 7206 1059 1 | £7.95 |
| **Edith Piaf** | *My Life* | 0 7206 1111 3 | £9.95 |
| **Marcel Proust** | *Pleasures and Regrets* | 0 7206 1110 5 | £9.95 |
| **Joseph Roth** | *Flight Without End* | 0 7206 1068 0 | £9.95 |
| **Joseph Roth** | *The Silent Prophet* | 0 7206 1135 0 | £9.95 |
| **Joseph Roth** | *Weights and Measures* | 0 7206 1136 9 | £9.95 |
| **Bram Stoker** | *Midnight Tales* | 0 7206 1134 2 | £9.95 |
| **Tarjei Vesaas** | *The Birds* | 0 7206 1143 1 | £9.95 |
| **Tarjei Vesaas** | *The Ice Palace* | 0 7206 1122 9 | £9.95 |

# PETER OWEN
## INDEPENDENT PUBLISHERS SINCE 1951

If you have enjoyed this book and would like to find out more about the books we publish or order a free catalogue, please contact:

The Sales Department
Peter Owen Publishers
73 Kenway Road
London SW5 0RE, UK

Tel: ++ **44 (0)20 7373 5628** or **7370 6093**
Fax: ++ **44 (0)20 7373 6760**
e-mail: **sales@peterowen.com**
or visit our website at: **www.peterowen.com**

## SOME AUTHORS WE HAVE PUBLISHED

James Agee • Tariq Ali • Guillaume Apollinaire • Machado de Assis • Miguel Angel Asturias • Thomas Blackburn • Jane Bowles • Paul Bowles • Lenny Bruce • Finn Carling • Blaise Cendrars • Marc Chagall • Uno Chiyo • Hugo Claus • Jean Cocteau • Albert Cohen • Colette • Margaret Crosland • e.e. cummings • Salvador Dalí • Osamu Dazai • Anita Desai • Fabián Dobles • William Donaldson • Autran Dourado • Lawrence Durrell • Isabelle Eberhardt • Sergei Eisenstein • Shusaku Endo • Erté • Knut Faldbakken • Ida Fink • Nicolas Freeling • André Gide • Natalia Ginzburg • Jean Giono • Johann Wolfgang von Goethe • William Goyen • Julien Gracq • Sue Grafton • Robert Graves • George Grosz • Barbara Hardy • H.D. • David Herbert • Gustaw Herling • Hermann Hesse • Shere Hite • King Hussein of Jordan • Abdullah Hussein • Grace Ingoldby • Yasushi Inoue • Ruth Inglis • Takeshi Kaiko • Anna Kavan • Yasunawi Kawabata • Nikos Kanzantzakis • James Kirkup • Paul Klee • Violette Leduc • Robert Liddell • Francisco García Lorca • Dacia Maraini • Guy de Maupassant • André Maurois • Henri Michaux • Henry Miller • Marga Minco • Yukio Mishima • Mohammed Mrabet • Gérard de Nerval • Anaïs Nin • Yoko Ono • Arto Paasilinna • Marco Pallis • Boris Pasternak • Cesare Pavese • Octavio Paz • Milorad Pavic • Mervyn Peake • Wendy Perriam • Edith Piaf • Fiona Pitt-Kethley • Ezra Pound • Marcel Proust • James Purdy • Jeremy Reed • Rodrigo Rey Rosa • Joseph Roth • Marquis de Sade • Cora Sandel • Jean-Paul Sartre • Gerald Scarfe • Albert Schweitzer • George Bernard Shaw • Isaac Bashevis Singer • Edith Sitwell • Stevie Smith • C.P. Snow • Vladimir Soloukhin • Natsume Soseki • Muriel Spark • Gertrude Stein • Bram Stoker • August Strindberg • Rabindranath Tagore • Tambimuttu • Roland Topor • Peter Vansittart • Tarjei Vesaas • Noel Virtue • Max Weber • William Carlos Williams • Monique Wittig • Alexander Zinoviev